WING AND A PRAYER

Wing and a Prayer

Cover Design by The Book Brander
TheBookBrander.com
Content Edits: Sue Brown-Moore
SueBrownMoore.com
Copy Edits: Laurel C. Kriegler
laurelckriegler.wordpress.com
Print Formatting by Nina Pierce of Seaside Publications
NinaPierce.com/book-formatting/

First Edition
ISBN: 979-8-9867802-1-4

WING AND A PRAYER

SILVERSTAR MATES

INTERGALACTIC DATING AGENCY

USA TODAY BESTSELLING AUTHOR

LEA KIRK

SFR by LEA KIRK

The Prophecy Series
(in chronological order)

Prophecy
Book One

Blue Christmas
A Prophecy Series Holiday Novella

Space Ranger
A Prophecy Series Short Story
(*newsletter exclusive*)

All of Me
A Prophecy Series Short Story

Salvation
Book Two

Collision
Book Three

Skylar's Gift
A Prophecy Series Novella

Paradox
(Coming Soon)

Silverstar Mates Series
(in recommended reading order)

Fly With Me
Above the Storm
Wing and a Prayer
Trial by Fire

PNR by LEA KIRK

Made for Her
Part of S. E. Smith's, The Worlds of Magic, New Mexico

ONE

Legally speaking, Meryl Faulkner was in a gray area, and that was not a good place for a retired divorce lawyer to be. She tapped the edge of her debit card against the grocery checkout counter. The whole situation wouldn't be quite so bad if she hadn't involved her goddaughter in her crime last night. But, if that damn man—because it was *always* a man—hadn't pissed her off so royally, she would've thought things through a little more carefully. Which wasn't an excuse because the facts spoke for themselves.

The first time she'd met the giant winged Bezchian lug, Rol Raptorclaw, she'd been all sorts of turned on. What guy his age could carry off the shirtless look so flawlessly? Had such defined abs? Looked so hot in nothing but leather flying straps and black pants? And spoke in a voice that could make a woman orgasm on the spot?

And those wings—my God.

But seriously, all that yumminess didn't make up for the way he'd tried to undermine his good friend Kyzel's budding romance with her best friend, Robyn. Poor Robyn deserved a chance to find a guy who was better than that damn ex-husband of hers, Kevin. And Kyzel was *exponentially* better.

Meryl had warned Rol to back off, but had he listened? Nooo. Of course not. Instead, he'd cornered Robyn during her lunch break yesterday and done everything to make her jealous of Kyzel's dead wife.

She frowned. And speaking of Robyn, her friend hadn't followed up with her today about that incident. Maybe she should drive by on her way home from the grocery store and make sure everything was okay. It was so unusual not to hear from her.

"Ms. Faulkner? Ma'am?"

Meryl blinked, the familiar electronic beeps and buzzes of the store filtering back into her consciousness. She met the expectant brown-eyed gaze of the grocery clerk. Cute young thing with hair done in neat cornrows.

I used to be that young. And cute.

The girl waved one hand in the direction of the ancient card reader. "You can tap your card now."

"Oh, right. Sorry." She set the card over the scanner.

What was the line from that movie? *"It's not the years, it's the mileage."* Sixty-three used to seem so far away, but now here she was, retired and just a couple years away from being a senior citizen.

She slipped her card back into her purse, then stared at the back of her hand. A few age spots were there, barely visible against her brown skin. It helped that she bleached her shoulder-length curls to a light-gold color. It hid the salt and pepper that only she knew was there. Not much she could do about the crow's feet at the corners of her eyes, though. Robyn called them laugh lines, but Robyn also managed to see the best in everyone.

Or, maybe she's right.

Life had been pretty happy. Even the disaster of a marriage to Nathan had been fun, despite her scare with cervical cancer, and the resulting hysterectomy that had stolen their ability to have a family. He had been there for her, strong and reassuring, for twenty-seven years. They'd lived their happily ever after until…Charlotte. Ditzy, petite, young Charlotte Cremean with her deep brown eyes, thick dark hair, and her equally thick head.

Totally missed all the signs on that one, didn't I?

Hadn't even batted an eyelash when Nathan wanted to hire her as their new secretary. Why would she have? She'd *trusted* him. Now all she had to show for those years were scars. A puckered one on her abdomen, and invisible ones on her heart. Did she need any other reminders how men liked to play women?

Aren'tcha glad you kept your last name now?

"Here's your receipt, ma'am."

Ma'am. I'm old enough to be a ma'am.

"Thank you." She took the receipt between her fingers and jammed it into the bag with the yogurt and bananas.

"Has anyone told you that you look like Michelle Hurd?"

She clamped down on the snort trying to escape. "So often that I could apply to be her stunt double and probably get the job."

Not that anyone would hire a "ma'am"-aged woman to do that job. Much easier to hire a younger, more flexible one and do distance shots.

"You could." The girl laughed. "Have a good evening."

"You too."

Out in the parking lot, the old wheels on the grocery cart rattled, and the whole contraption shimmied. Damn thing better not fall apart on her before she got to the car. How was it that ten years after first contact was made, asphalt was still a thing? Didn't one of the other planets that belonged to the Galactic Alliance have a better surfacing solution they could share with Earth?

A whole decade, yet the first time I met an off-worlder was only a few days ago.

And what was it about Rol that kept him floating to the forefront of her thoughts all the time? The dignified gray and brown headfeathers and wings? His buff as a twenty-five-year-old's body? Which sort of made sense since a spare tire would make flying difficult. Or those eyes...one gray and one blue...that she could stare into for hours... days... months...*years*?

Dammit. Don't think about him like that!

She stopped behind her sporty little silver coupe and loaded her bags into the trunk. Rol was a dick, and she'd wronged him for it by having her goddaughter, Kathy hack into the Silverstar Agency's database, submit a fake application for him, then bio apped one of his feathers to them as well. And that damn feather was *still* in her purse. Why? Because it smelled all allspicey-warm, like Rol, and she couldn't let it go.

Who's the dick now, Meryl? Ma'am?

She rolled the empty cart into the rack. He'd be so pissed if he ever found out what she'd done to him. If she was really lucky, he'd be back on Bezchi long before the agency matched him, and the whole thing would blow over. As hard as it was to admit it, she'd let down all womankind with her petty little stunt.

And yet, just the thought of him leaving made her heart sad. It was beyond crazy, but she might be hooked on the guy, which was another thing he could never know.

She slid behind the steering wheel, the bucket seat conforming to her ass. The cheery notes of The Wedding March came from inside her purse, and her stomach clenched. It'd seemed funny to give that ringtone to Nixy Vogel, the Silverstar agent assigned to her. Now, not so much.

This could be the call I've been dreading.

The one she'd known would eventually come the moment Robyn had coerced her into submitting an application with her. It wasn't like *she* needed a guy in her life again. Why, oh why didn't she think to have Kathy delete her application last night?

"Well, Nixy, honey, leave a message." It was getting dark, and she still wanted to drive by Robyn's to make sure her bestie was home and safe.

Anything Nixy had to tell her could wait until after the groceries were put away.

TWO

———————✳———————

Four days later.

The desert sun beat down on Rol Raptrclaw's wings, glaring off the white sands and heating the old, cracked black asphalt of Earth's galactic spaceport. Had Earth's Intergalactic Relations and Commerce committee not negotiated for better surfacing materials from one of the other planets in the Alliance? He gave his head a shake. Not his concern. Soon he would board the ship bound for Bezchi, along with his monarchs, Kyzel, and Kyzel's new mate, Robyn Martin.

Soon.

Right after Kyzel and Robyn finished their little lover's reunion at the end of the ship's boarding ramp. In plain sight of everyone. Including Robyn's youngest daughter, Kathy and best friend, Meryl.

How long could two people kiss like that, anyway? They *must* be aware that they would have two days in space to get it out of their systems before arriving on Bezchi. He fought the urge to roll his eyes in a manner unbecoming of the prime advisor to the monarchs of the Raptorclaw clan. The Bezchian contingent—including himself, Kyzel's body-guard, Fyad, and the phoenix mate-matcher, Elder Kai Firewing—all patiently waited for Kyzel and Robyn.

Well, he and Fyad did. Elder Kai looked like he had eaten something sour. Not that Rol did not have some empathy for the elder. It was awkward standing by waiting, especially with Meryl standing no more than two wingspans away from him.

You only have yourself to blame.

It was, after all, he who had facilitated this reunion by sneaking off to Robyn's house this morning and convincing the stubborn human that she did not need to *be* Bezchian to serve their people—and hers.

Lucky for him, she had seen the truth of the matter and come along willingly. If she had not, he had been prepared to scoop her up and fly her to the spaceport anyway. Such an action *could* be classified as an abduction, but his choices had been limited. The sorrow shrouding Kyzel had been too much to bear because Kyzel was not only his monarch; he was his friend.

"Oh, lighten up, Rol." Meryl's melodious voice drew him back to the present.

He gave her a sidelong glare. She had been a burr in his wing since he had first encountered her one Earth-week ago. It was a shame, too, as she was quite tolerable when she was not speaking to him. "I am unfamiliar with this saying, Ms. Faulkner."

Meryl smirked and the fine lines at the corners of her eyes deepened. "It means, don't be such a tight-ass. A little spontaneity is good for the soul."

What was more spontaneous than flying Ms. Martin out here without his monarch's knowledge or blessing? This time he did roll his eyes skyward. The young human female standing next to Meryl giggled. Robyn's daughter, Kathy happened to also be related to Meryl by an Earth ritual called *baptism*. How unfortunate for the youngling.

And how callous of you to even think such a thing.

Since meeting her, Meryl had shown the capacity to care deeply for those she loved. He just did not happen to be included in that select group, for whatever reason.

No, the reason was plain: he had not *earned* that designation in her life. He may have even revolted against it on some unconscious level.

He shifted his gaze to Elder Kai Firewing. The Firewing clan's main function was to match mating pairs within the other four Bezchian clans. It was an ancient tradition that they had upheld for thousands upon thousands of sun migrations.

Oh, there had been a few exceptions, of course. Kyzel had just done the unthinkable by eschewing that tradition and finding his new mate through the services of the Silverstar Agency on Earth. And about fifteen sun migrations ago, a Raptorclaw ship's captain had liberated a pirate ship of its Earthling *cargo*, then mated with one of the females.

Ava Raptorclaw. Dear, sweet, pain-in-the-wing, Ava. If not for her, the Galactic Alliance of Planets would not have bothered making first contact with Earth ten sun migrations ago.

And then there is me.

Unmateable, because of weakened genes. An affliction

all could see each time they looked into his dual-tone eyes. One gray, one blue.

The sound of footsteps on metal intruded on his thoughts. Kyzel and Robyn had ended their kiss while he was distracted, and she was saying her goodbyes to her daughter and her best friend.

He slid his gaze back to Meryl. Her brown skin was covered with a thin sheen of moisture, almost glowing under the midday desert sun. Even her hair—dark at the roots, but golden at the ends—shimmered like fire in the sunlight.

Meryl Faulkner *was* fire, in her appearance and in her personality. Touch her, and he might get burned. But, if he *could* touch her, just once, it might be worth the pain. Even though the female seemed perpetually exasperated with him.

Ah, well, it was not meant to be. Despite both of them being past prime heir-providing years, he was still not an acceptable choice as a mate.

Finally, the newly mated pair strolled up the ramp, hand in hand. He stepped forward, keeping his gaze firmly on his monarchs, not Meryl. Kyzel had stopped midway up the ramp, turned, and now stared at him with an expression of stunned disbelief, a human cell phone in his hand. Rol frowned. Was that the same one the Silverstar agent, Nixy Vogel had given him the day they had arrived?

Rol made a vague hand-wave in the direction of the phone. "Did you forget to return the device, *kee mohap*?"

Probably had it in one of the carrying pouches of his flying leathers. Surely, Meryl would return it, if asked.

Kyzel shook his head. "Rol, you did not tell me you had applied to the Silverstar Agency."

9

A shiver of surprise went through his wings. Applied? To Silverstar? *What*?

Rol squinted at the ship taxiing toward the launch pad. The ship he *should* be on right now, but because of the most bizarre circumstance, he was not.

How by the ever-loving eternals did the Silverstar Agency get my name?

In truth, the how did not matter, because he was staying on Earth to meet his *match*. His refusal to do so could affect the up-coming trade negotiations between Bezchi and Earth, and not in a positive way. He had personally put great effort into making them happen to begin with.

Kyzel would not have submitted his name in revenge for the way he had attempted to dissuade Robyn from pursuing a relationship with his monarch, would he? A wave of shame chased the suspicion away. How could he even think such about his childhood friend? Kyzel had never been a revenge seeker, and never would be.

A rumble, followed by a wavering heat mirage billowing from under the ship brought his focus back to the space craft.

"There they go." Kathy slid her arm around Meryl's waist and the two leaned against each other in family solidarity.

"Are you ready to go, Prime Advisor?" Kyzel's bodyguard, Fyad grinned. His black-as-night headfeathers and wings glistened in the intense sunlight.

The youngling seemed unusually pleased at the prospect

of continuing his duties on Earth. This time to protect Rol and Elder Kai.

Rol cast one final glance at the microscopic black dot ascending through the blue sky. He would be able to see the shuttle better if he used his hunting vision, but why bother? Gone was gone.

"I am ready." He had a meeting to attend with Ms. Vogel in an hour. "Elder Kai, will you fly with us?"

Kai Firewing flexed his silvery-red wings. "Aye. We have delayed long enough."

Rol frowned as the elder—who was close to fifteen sun migrations older than his sixty—tromped toward a patch of open ground with room enough to take off. Could it have been Kai who submitted his name? It made no logical sense, but the male *had* manipulated him into tricking Robyn to believe untruths about Kyzel, a plot designed to end their courtship and get the raptor monarch to submit to a traditional match on Bezchi.

Yes, he understood Meryl's outrage about that now. It had been a foolish thing to do.

"Rol?" And speaking of Meryl....

He turned his gaze to the irritating and beguiling female. "Yes?"

"Thank you for getting Robyn out here before Kyzel left." She made a shrugging gesture with her hands. "I appreciate it."

He suppressed the smile of satisfaction at the notion he had done *something* right in her eyes. Instead, he raised his chin a bit and gazed down his nose at her. "You are welcome."

11

Convincing Robyn that Kyzel was her true mate, then bringing her to the spaceport, was a point of pride. Of all his accomplishments as prime advisor, few had left him with the warm glow that now resided in his chest.

If nothing else, he had proved to Meryl that, despite her vague threats of retaliation for his role in Robyn's eventual kidnapping by her ex-mate, he *did* care.

Meryl's green-brown gaze did not waver, and she smiled. A soft puff of a breeze fluttered her sleeveless yellow top, molding it over her small breasts and flat belly. But what really held his attention was the glimpse of her soul in her eyes. There must be more to her under her shell of contrariness. It was too bad he would never have the opportunity to find out.

"Prime," Fyad rumbled, a hint of agitation in his voice. "The elder has left without us."

"Let him go, Fyad." For some reason, this did not trouble him, even though he should be a little more concerned about an old phoenix on his own on an unfamiliar planet.

Fyad lifted his wings a little higher without opening them. "Monarch Kyzel charged me to watch over *both* of you, Prime Advisor."

This was true. "Very well. It was an honor to meet you, Meryl Faulkner...Ms. Kathy."

He gave each woman a bow of respect. Kathy's words were lost to him as he strode away, but Meryl's murmured ones were clear.

"See ya soon."

If only there was a valid reason to do so. But there was not. He quickened his pace, faster and faster until he was running.

Then pumped his wings and jumped, taking to the hot desert air currents. Ah, it was tempting to circle back for just one last glimpse of the human beauty, but she might notice.

It took next to no time to catch up with Elder Kai, and the remainder of the flight from the desert back over the mountains into the Imperial Valley took less than half of an Earth hour. The sheer number of humans populating the area was evident by the nearly unbroken line of structures stretching from the San Jacinto mountain range to the blue waters called the Pacific Ocean. Nests, called *houses* here, were set in groupings between places of business. And in the far distance were the incredible *skyscrapers* of Los Angeles. Including the twin knife-blade-like towers of the Earth's Intergalactic Relations and Commerce buildings.

He would have to make time to attend some of the trade negotiation sessions once they started, per Kyzel's request. After all, he had been instrumental in convincing the Bezchian Trade Guild that commerce with Earth could be beneficial.

Rol hovered above the Silverstar Agency's five-storey building as Elder Kai alighted on the roof. Then the elder walked briskly toward the wide, arched entryway.

"After you, Prime Advisor," Fyad said from where he floated at Rol's right.

Rol waved one hand in Kai's direction. "Why did he choose to stay on Earth, do you suppose?"

Fyad shrugged his shoulders, smooth dark skin rippled over his ropey muscles. "Who knows the reasons of the Firewing elders. But I suspect he will make my life difficult."

Elder Kai disappeared into the building and Rol snorted. "Our monarch has given you quite a mission to fulfill."

Fyad flashed a cocky grin full of youthful confidence. "Nothing more than I can handle, Prime Advisor."

Of course not. Rol dipped one wing and dropped into a controlled spiral to the roof. A moment later, his sandaled feet touched the thick patch of green lawn that served as the landing pad, and he folded his wings. Fyad glided in next to him, also pulling in his black wings. Together they made their way inside and took the elevator down a floor to the travelers' nest—or suite, in English—assigned to them.

Rol strode through the doorway and allowed himself an internal sigh. What a bland and tiresome place these rooms had become. Oh, it was spacious enough, easily accommodating the three of them—four when Kyzel had been there. The furnishings were minimal, which made it less likely that anything would be tipped over by their wings in a moment of inattention. But it had too few windows, and no direct access to the outside.

He sighed and lowered his wings a fraction. "I thought I had seen the last of this place."

Yet, here he was again. May the immortals help him if he figured out who had submitted his name. He would defeather them. Slowly. Painfully. One shaft at a time.

Fyad entered behind him. "It could be worse, Prime Advisor."

"How could it possibly be worse, Fyad?"

"I...do not know, exactly." Fyad furrowed his brow below his widow's peak.

Rol gave the young guard an exasperated frown. "Then

why did you say so?"

"It is what Earthlings say." Fyad shrugged his shoulders, making his black flying harness creak. "It seems to make them feel better."

Oh, the Earthlings said it, so it *must* help. "You have been here too long."

"Correction." Elder Kai shuffled in the direction of the wide archway in the center of the back wall that was the entrance to the sleeping accommodations. "He has spent too much time with the locals."

"I have not." Fyad fluffed his wings with a huff.

Great Aerie, give him patience. "It is almost two o'clock. I am going downstairs to meet with Ms. Vogel."

The elder reversed trajectory next to the tall dining table and headed back toward him. "I will go with you."

"You are not coming with me, Elder Kai."

Kai stopped, his expression as petulant as a fledgling being denied a sweet. "Why not?"

"Because, this is a personal matter between me and Ms. Vogel." Until he understood the nature of this incident, it was best Kai stay here. Nothing good came from annoying Ms. Vogel, or any female, for that matter. And rumor had it that Firewing had already annoyed the human mate-matcher enough.

"Pah." Kai waved his hand in Fyad's direction. "Bring my luggage back to my room, youngling."

The corner of Rol's mouth twitched, and he tamped down on the urge to laugh. Instead, he exchanged a glance with Fyad, then mouthed, "Watch him," before making his way through the doorway.

THREE

Two days later.

Rol prowled the circumference of theTerrace Cabana's interior. It was one of the few bar-restaurant establishments in the area with a wide enough front entrance for him to fit, which made it the most convenient place to meet his so-called match for the first time. Plus, this place had a picturesque terrace overlooking the beach and the Pacific Ocean. All that was why he had agreed when Ms. Vogel had suggested it.

He huffed. Ms. Vogel was a secretive little human. And so, apparently, was his human match. Mysterious, divorced, and lacked a brood of younglings. That was all he knew about her…except that she would be wearing a green shirt and black leggings. The actual description involved more precise wording like *teal* and *slacks*, but what did it matter?

As long as she is not one of those females who carries a tiny dog in her purse.

It was a strange custom, pet carrying. But Ms. Vogel had not indicated his match would have anything in particular in her black *clutch*, other than a Silverstar business card.

A gentle breeze flowed through the open glass-paned doors at the rear of the establishment. The clean scent of the ocean wafted around him, fluttering the fabric of his *omlek*. The loose Bezchian style shirt draped over him and laced up his sides. It covered his chest and back while accommodating his wings, leaving them unhindered.

No one would accuse him of repeating Kyzel's mistake of not covering himself with anything more than flying leathers during his first visit with Robyn. What a fiasco that had been. Despite the ridiculousness of Rol's situation, it was important to respect the sensibilities of human females.

He stepped through the doorway onto a spacious wooden deck. Only a handful of humans were out there enjoying the late afternoon sun, and all of them turned as one and stared at him. As usual. Like an off-worlder visiting their little planet was something new.

He gazed back at them with cool detachment. None of the females were dressed in the outfit Ms. Vogel had described for his date, although one did have a dog in her purse.

He moved toward an unoccupied tall table at the far end and slid onto the perch—*stool*. Since he was stuck here until he had made an honorable attempt to fulfill an obligation he had never signed up for, the least he could do was try to use the proper English words.

"Can I get you a drink?"

Rol focused his attention on the young waitress with hair the color of the sand on the beach, and an upturned nose covered with little spots called *freckles*. "Water for now, thank you."

"Are you waiting for someone?"

"Yes, I am."

"Two waters, then?"

Having water for his date would show consideration. "Yes, two please."

"Okay. My name is Savannah, and I'll be right back." She walked away, her pale ponytail swaying from side to side as though waving farewell.

He gave his wings a gentle shake and settled them close to his back, then cast his attention out over the beach and the sparkling blue waves of the Pacific Ocean. All right, he was here early, and ready to at least *try* to like this unknown female. But the agency was wrong. No female would take him as a mate, not even a human.

A furtive movement drew his attention to a row of surfboards stored side by side against a special structure made for them. He blinked slowly to lower his hunting vision lenses—the extra eye coverings left over from his ancestors' days. Someone was behind the boards making slow methodical motions as though wiping the boards clean. Brilliant invention, those surfboards. Gliding on the waves must feel almost like gliding through the air above them.

The under-feathers at the base of his skull ruffled and a pleasant vibration ran down his spine. Someone familiar was nearby. A faint citrusy scent set his mouth to watering. He blinked away his hunting vision and turned his head toward the open doorway. The tall, slim, golden-curled, sable-skinned beauty in the doorway was all too familiar, and it seemed like the rest of the bar faded into obscurity.

Meryl's gaze met his, and her expression changed to a resigned smirk. And *that* was why it would never work between them. He took in a deep breath and blew it out through his nose as she sauntered over.

"Well, well, well." Her casual smile seemed somewhat forced. "Imagine meeting you here."

"Yes. Imagine." What were the odds that they would be in the same bar at the same time after all?

She pointed to the chair directly across the table from him. "May I?"

"Of course." The urge to glance back at the doorway was strong on the chance his match had followed her in, but that might be misconstrued as rude. There was no point in giving her ammunition if there was a chance for them to have a civil conversation. "And what brings you here?"

Her gaze swept away from his to focus on her fidgeting fingers wrapped around her black-leather bag. "Waiting for someone."

"As am I. I do not think it would be inappropriate for us to wait together, then." What had possessed him to say such a thing?

She seemed to vacillate, then nodded. "Sure, why not?"

There was so much economic grace in her movements, no motion without purpose. Even the way she placed her bag on the table seemed intentional.

"So." She gave him an expectant look. "How are our friends doing? They should be to Bezchi by now."

"Oh, good." Savannah popped into existence. She set a tall glass of ice water in front of Meryl, then him. "You're both here now. Can I get you anything from the bar? Drinks? Maybe some of our house-made pretzels?"

Meryl shifted on her stool, her folded hands in her lap now the center of her attention.

He forced down the urge to correct Savannah about his

relationship with Meryl. "One of your hard ciders, please."

He had discovered this glorious beverage while Kyzel was getting acquainted with his mate. The smoky-sweet flavor never failed to bring back memories of a similar brew on Bezchi.

"Got it. Ma'am?"

Meryl waved one hand. "Pretzels sound great, and I'll have a margarita on whole ice, with salt."

Savannah grinned. "Excellent." She tucked her pen and notepad into her apron pocket. "Be right back."

Once they were alone again, Meryl rested her crossed forearms on the table. "You were saying?"

"No, I have not spoken to Kyzel since yesterday." Ever since his friend had ordered him to stop reporting in every day. And something about a *honeymoon*, whatever that was.

"Well, damn."

"You have not heard from Ms. Donah—Robyn, then?" Kyzel's mate had not hesitated to use Bezchian law to drop her ex-mate's name. As far as he was aware, she planned to claim Raptorclaw once Bezchi officially recognized her mating to Kyzel.

It was a strange practice, these last names Earthlings had. On Bezchi, there were no last names, only clan names. In his case, he was Rol of Raptorclaw, or Rol Raptorclaw. Or just Prime Advisor to the Raptorclaw clan's monarchs.

"No, I haven't heard from her." She pinched the end of her straw between her fingers and moved it in a circular motion. The ice in her water tinkled as it tapped the side of her glass. "I don't have a deep-space communicator."

"You do not?"

She met his gaze finally, and raised her eyebrows at him. "They don't exactly sell those at the corner store, y'know."

No, he did not know. But he would keep that little piece of ignorance to himself. He gave her a measured nod instead. "I see."

"I wish they did, though."

As did he, because an idea had squirmed into his brain that was not at all in his best interest.

"It'd make Kathy so happy to talk to her mom." Meryl smiled, the way she always seemed to when talking about her goddaughter.

"I see." It was such a versatile and neutral response.

"And so would Robyn's other kids, Karen and Kevin, Jr." She shrugged her narrow shoulders. "They didn't really get to say goodbye."

Rol frowned. "They did agree to her departure, though."

Encouraged her, in fact. Kevin, Jr. had even referred to it as a "well-deserved gift" for his mother.

"Well, yeah, but it doesn't mean they don't miss her." A light breeze ruffled over her hair.

He tightened his grip around his thighs to keep his hands from reaching out and smoothing a stray strand back into place.

"I see your point." *Keep your mouth sealed and do not offer anything.* "I have a portable deep-space communicator at the travelers' nest."

A groan lodged in his throat. Despite his efforts, the offer had slipped out anyway.

"The…travelers' nest?"

"The *suite* Silverstar provided us." Where most of their off-world clients stayed until they were matched.

21

"Oh? Are you offering to let us use it?"

No. "Yes."

"Here's your drinks." Savannah sounded far too cheery as she set the beverages on the table.

The knot of tension forming between his wing blades tightened a little bit more.

"Thank you, Savannah." Meryl's smile was bright enough to light the entire terrace, if it were not in the full mid-afternoon sun already.

"You're welcome." She placed a basket of miniature pretzels between them. "Can I get you anything else?"

The bready aroma wafted up from the freshly baked pretzels and a long, loud growl came from his stomach.

Meryl smirked. "Rol might want to see the dinner menu soon."

"No—"

"I'll get it." And the girl was gone, hopping away like an excited chick.

Had he ever had that much energy even as a fledgling?

A throaty chuckle brought his attention back to Meryl. "What?"

"Nothing."

Oh, it was something. Her knowing grin said so.

Meryl shook her head. "Isn't she a little young for you?"

He blinked, twice. Was she insinuating...? "That is an incredibly rude assumption, Ms. Faulkner."

Now it was her turn to blink. The confusion on her face filled him with righteous satisfaction. Good, she recognized how wholly unacceptable it would be for him to lust after such a young—

"Lighten up, Rol. You wouldn't be the first guy to succumb to the charms of a younger woman."

Did he detect a current of bitterness in her words? "Such a liaison would be improper, unless we had been matched by an elder."

And even then, the mere thought of being with such a young female was disturbing.

"Okay, okay. I'm sorry. I won't do it again."

"Then I will overlook your mistake."

"That's big of you." She raised her glass, took a long sip, then ran her tongue over her dark red lips.

He swallowed, hard, unable to look away. Cursed currents of air, he was getting turned on. By *Meryl Faulkner*. Talk about improper.

The clack of her glass on the tabletop broke the spell.

She smiled in a disarming way. "So, I can use your deep-space communicator?

Communicator? Ah, yes. The offer had been made, and there was no getting out of this now.

He brought the cider bottle to his mouth and let the cool heady beverage slide down his throat. It was a stalling tactic. Now that Meryl knew about the device, she would pummel him with her non-existent wings until he relented.

He lowered the bottle and met her gaze. "Yes."

"Thank—"

"But," he raised one hand. "You must arrange its usage with me in advance. Elder Kai shares the suite with Fyad and me, and I will not have him inconvenienced."

"Deal." She had the biggest most beautiful smile. "How about this weekend?"

"You and Ms. Kathy are welcome then."

Her smile turned sly. "I *may* have invited Karen and Kev out for a visit."

May have? "Well, did you?"

"What?"

"Invite them?"

She blinked her wide hazel eyes at him, then laughed. "Yes. The minute I found out you had the communicator, which was the day Robyn left."

"You deceived me."

"I out-maneuvered you." She leaned forward. "C'mon, Rol, you would've done the same for your family."

True, he would have for his mother. Possibly for his father too, if his sire had not already worked himself into an early flight to the Great Aerie. The price of trying to escape the disappointment of a defective heir. "Very well, then. We can arrange a time after they arrive."

"Sounds good." Meryl turned her glass on the tabletop in increments. "So."

"So?"

She dipped her chin and raise her eyebrows in a way that suggested he was missing something important. "You haven't figured it out yet?"

"Figured what out?"

"Your Silverstar date?" She caught her full lower lip between her teeth, drawing his attention back to her mouth.

Why did Earth females paint their lips anyway? Meryl was lovely without the coloring, more natural. Although, the green of her silky sleeveless shirt did compliment her hazel eyes.

Wait...*green* shirt? Ms. Vogel said his date would be wearing a green shirt. And...he leaned to his right to peer under the table, his gaze snagging on the hem of Meryl's *black* leggings.

"Impossible." And why had he not noticed sooner? He straightened and locked gazes with her. "This cannot be."

"Ouch." She flipped a Silverstar business card between her fingers as if she had pulled it out of thin air. "But, in all fairness, that's pretty much what I said when Nixy told me."

How? How could this over-bearing, meddling female *possibly* be his match?

FOUR

———————✳———————

Well now, this had just turned into the clusterfuck of the century. Meryl's only consolation was that Rol seemed as surprised by the match as she'd been when Nixy had told her. Talk about karma coming back and biting her in the ass.

"But this must be a mistake." Rol was so solidly in the denial phase.

At least she'd had a few days longer to process it. Even so, she'd gotten to the tavern early today to get a drink under her belt before she chickened out. That plan had crashed and burned because he had beat her here.

"That's *another* thing I said to Nixy."

He rested his forearms on the table's edge and leaned toward her. "How long have you known?"

"Since the day after Robyn called me to pick her up from that rest stop." She slid Nixy's card back into her clutch.

"That was *last week*."

"I *know*."

Rol shook his head in disbelief, the glints of gray in his headfeathers catching in the sunlight. "You knew even when we were at the galactic spaceport."

It wasn't a question, but she nodded anyway.

"And you would have let me go home without saying anything?"

It did sound awful selfish of her when he put it that way. "Would you have believed me?"

He rotated his cider bottle in circles and frowned.

"I didn't think so." She raised her glass to her lips and took another sip of her margarita. Rol tracked her movements with his eyes. How could someone so sexy be such a pain in the ass? "When you ended up staying, I had to call Nixy quick and ask her not to tell you who I was."

It was more like a threat: *Tell him and I'll cancel the date and my application.* Nixy hadn't been too happy about it, but once she'd understood their contentious relationship, she'd accepted her terms.

"Why did you do so?"

And that was the million-dollar question, wasn't it? "I don't know."

He tilted his head to one side and peered at her with obvious curiosity. "Any regrets, now?"

Misgivings still, but not outright regrets. He'd still be pissed once she told him the truth about how Silverstar got his name. May as well get that revelation over with. She took in a deep breath.

A woman's scream from the beach tore her attention away from Rol. Sounded like someone was in trouble.

Something big and black and winged rose up from behind a row of vertical surfboards holding a struggling figure in his arms. "Is that a…. Holy *shit*. Isn't that the guard guy Kyzel left behind with you?"

Rol had his hand pressed to his forehead and his teeth clenched. "Yes. That is Fyad."

"Oh my God." One of the women on the terrace pointed. "That off-worlder is *abducting* a woman."

It sure looked that way. And the apparent abduction was being carried out by a Bezchian. "Rol. What's he *thinking*?"

"I do not know." His large fists rested on the table as if he was trying not to pound them through the opaque glass.

A movement behind him at the opposite end of the deck drew her gaze. A Schwarzenegger-sized guy had abandoned his stool, and his date—and his date's little yappy dog—and was storming in their direction.

She slid off her own stool and rested one hand on Rol's forearm. "You gotta get out of here."

He gave her a confused look. "Why?"

"Hey you, *alien*," Schwarzenegger-guy shouted.

"*That's* why." No one used the term alien anymore, except as a slur.

Rol, being Rol, stood to face the threat.

Schwarz didn't slow down, even though Rol had a good six inches on him. "What the hell, man? Your kind are stealing our women now?"

Oh geez. Now people from inside the bar were crowding into the open doorway, and they didn't look too happy either.

She moved to stand between Rol and Schwarz. "No. He's not…*they're* not. Bezchians have more honor than that."

One of the women at the next table snorted. "Sure doesn't look that way."

"I know." It really looked bad, actually. She turned to face Rol. "That's why *my friend* here is going after them."

Rol's eyes widened. "I am?"

"Yes." She gave his arm a tug and moved toward the steps leading to the beach. "You are. And you're going to find out what What's-his-name is up to, and *fix it*."

He rolled his eyes but didn't resist, following along like an obedient puppy. Schwarz and company glared, expectant but seemingly willing to let her handle the situation. At least for now. That dog, on the other hand, was still yapping, hanging halfway out of its purse as if saying, *Hold me back, man.* Obviously, it was the only one smart enough to see right through her ploy.

At the bottom step, Rol bent and removed his shoes. "Are you coming with me?" he murmured.

"Someone's gotta pay the tab." She wasn't about to stiff poor Savannah.

"Allow me to contribute." He clipped his shoes onto his belt, then reached into his pants pocket and pulled out a wad of cash.

"Goddamn, Rol, put that away." She grabbed his hand between hers. "You can pay me back later."

"I—"

"Don't worry about it. We'll figure it out. Right now, you gotta go before things get out of hand."

"Very well." He shoved the cash back into his pocket. "Good day to you, then, Ms. Faulkner."

"Yeah. See ya, Raptorclaw." Shit. They'd have to see each other again, and it was her fault.

But she *did* want to know what Fyad was up to, and who the woman was.

Rol turned and ran across the sand toward the water, muscles rippling under his skin-hugging black leggings. Each stride lengthening the distance between them faster and faster until he unfurled his massive wings.

Her breath caught at the beauty of the sunlight glistening over his fully extended feathered appendages, and she pressed her hand to her chest. He leaped into the air, his muscles rolling and straining as his bulk defied gravity, then he was airborne. There was nothing quite as impressive as a Bezchian taking flight. Even the dog must agree because it'd finally shut up.

She watched until he banked north, the direction Fyad had gone with that poor woman. And just like that the excitement was over. Patrons made their ways back to their seats, a few casting a parting glare at her. Whatever. There was nothing more she could do now except pay the tab then find some dinner. Once again, she'd be eating on her own.

What the hell had Nixy been thinking?

FIVE

It was late, and dark. And there was nothing worse than flying in the dark on this tech-starved planet. Too many tall buildings, towers, and wires—and the occasional aircraft.

I hope Ms. Faulkner appreciates the risks I took to find my wayward bodyguard.

The bodyguard who was still missing. But there was only so much that could be done at this late hour. Hunting vision did not work well in the dark, and he did not have night vision as some in his clan did.

He alighted on the roof of the Silverstar building and entered. At least the travelers' nest would be warm. Early autumn days on this part of Earth were beautifully hot, but the nights.... A shiver rippled along his wings. The moment the sun went below the horizon, an uncomfortable chill set in.

As he approached the doors to the suite he shared with Fyad and Elder Kai, they slid open. A wave of heat blasted out and he almost staggered back a step. He had expected it to be warm, but not like the Bezchian desert in the summer.

"Elder Kai?" He barked the name with more force than he had intended.

A movement drew his gaze to the figure huddled on a tall stool. The elder sat hunched over the waist-high dining table. The familiar deep purple eyes set in the pale leathery face peered at him. "Aye? Is something wrong, Prime Advisor?"

Many things were wrong at this point, but all of them faded in importance to the wan appearance of the elder. "It is sweltering in here. Are you ill?"

"No." Kai waved one long-fingered hand. "I discovered things today that left me yearning for home. You may readjust the internal room temperature if you like."

That he could understand. The Firewing elders did live in one of the hottest climates on Bezchi, and Kai was close to fifteen sun migrations his senior. It would be selfish to begrudge the old mate-matcher his comforts.

"Not to worry, Elder." He moved into the common room. "I will manage."

Kai tilted his head, concern flashed in his eyes. "You have a problem, Prime. It flows from you like an aura."

There was very little anyone could hide from a Firewing's empathic abilities.

"More than one problem, actually." He settled on the perch across the table from the old man.

"Oh? Can an elderly elder assist?"

"I am not certain." The last time this particular elder had advised him, it had gotten him into a lot of trouble.

"Pah, of course I can." Kai leaned forward, chest against the table's edge. "Especially if one of your problems involves a female. I do know a thing or two about matches."

Bitter resentment coated the back of his throat. "As you know, I am unmateable, Elder."

"Not according to that so-called matching agency downstairs." Was that a glint of disgust in the old male's eyes?

The urge to sneer at the elder for the way his kind had kept him single and heirless bubbled in his gut. "My match from the Silverstar Agency is none other than Meryl Faulkner."

Kai's eyes widened. "Ms. Donahue's friend?"

"Yes." He placed his elbows on the table and shoved his fingers through his cap of feathers. "It is a disaster."

As much as he wished to point out to the elder that *someone* thought he was worthy of a mate, he held it in.

"The match, or this afternoon's meeting?"

"Both."

Elder Kai sighed. "I understand your frustration. I also question the process involved in their results, but you would not turn away from a match made by a Firewing elder based on one meeting, would you?"

"No." He met the elder's gaze. "Have elder-made matches ever failed?"

"Seldom." Kai shrugged. "But neither mate is released from their match until they have made an honest try. As much as I disagree with Silverstar, I must remind you that you are a male of honor."

Which was a point of personal pride. "My other problem is that Fyad stole a human female off the beach this afternoon, and I have been unable to locate him."

"That, I can help you with." Kai sat up straighter, looking pleased. "He is in his room."

Every muscle in his body tightened to full alert. "He *is*?"

"He landed just after sunset."

So he, Rol, had been flapping around in the dark risking life and wing for no reason? He curled his hands into fists. That was unacceptable. He pushed out of the perch.

"Prime." The warning in the elder's voice caught his attention. "He has *company*."

"Company?" What did that mean?

Kai gave him a pointed look. "Possibly your missing female—"

A muffled shriek and a pounding sound came from the direction of the hallway to the bedrooms. "That does not sound like *willing* company."

"No." The elder lowered his gaze to the tabletop. "She did not seem too happy when they landed either. But she was not complaining at that time, so I did not interfere."

The situation could not be ignored, then. He strode into the hallway—the noticeably cooler hallway, thank the immortals. Kai had only fiddled with the common room's thermostat.

He came to a stop in front of Fyad's door. It did not open for him as it should have.

Elder Kai appeared at his side. "Locked."

"How observant." He pressed his lips together and rubbed one hand over his jaw.

Fyad had no business locking it. As prime advisor and the ranking Bezchian here, he was entitled to access to all parts of the suite, including the private rooms.

"You can't keep me here," the female's voice shouted from the other side. "It's illegal."

That did not sound good.

"And publishing lies is not?" Fyad's words were heavily laced with sarcasm.

"That's perception, and freedom of the press."

"You had no right."

"It's my job."

"There is no honor in your job."

That was enough. He raised his fist and pounded it against the door, the booms echoing in the corridor. "Open now, Fyad."

Silence settled over the enclosed area. He narrowed his glare at the wide, sliding double doors. If only they were transparent, if for no other reason than to show his displeasure to his bodyguard.

Bodyguard...or fledgling? Where was the mature, experienced guard who Kyzel had left here?

Swoosh.

The doors parted to reveal the two occupants: Fyad with his hands clenched into fists at his sides, black wings held high, feathers fluffed with agitation as he glared down at a familiar Earth female. The female glared back, arms crossed and chin lifted. Both were blazingly perfect examples of two people who would not back down regardless of how wrong—or right—they might be.

The woman's short, darker-than-night hair shimmered under the ceiling lights almost matching the jet black of Fyad's wings. It was extraordinary how much the two younglings appeared like a matched set. And was that the problem? They were too much alike?

"Still there." Kai's murmur came from behind him, but

35

the elder did not seem inclined to expound on his comment.

It was just as well. The last thing this situation needed was any more potential fuel.

"I'm leaving now," the female announced.

Fyad shook his head. "No, you are not."

The woman turned her angry gaze toward Rol. "Your guy here kidnapped me and is now keeping me here against my wil—"

"She was taking unsanctioned pictures of you and Ms. Faulkner."

Great Aerie, help him. This sounded like the squabbles that erupted between Kyzel's fledglings from time to time. Rol pulled his wings snug against his back, the ends of his primary feathers brushing his calves as he mentally counted backward from five. How had Kyzel and Careene tolerated it?

He returned the woman's gaze. "I remember you now. You are with that publication…."

"Raven Crawford, photographer for *Blast off!*, and a reporter now, too." She pointed a finger at Fyad. "And your boy here is in big trouble once *this* story gets out."

Bad publicity on Earth was not something Bezchi could afford. Especially with the upcoming trade negotiations.

Meryl. How had he been matched with *her*? It was…unfathomable. And why was *that* situation coming to mind now when his focus should be on the issue at wing…Fyad's human reporter?

He gave himself a mental shake, then raised his chin and glowered down at Raven. "I propose a compromise."

One of Raven's thin eyebrows arched upward. "What's that?"

"A...compromise? It is a deal, a mutual agreement." What else would it be called in her language?

Raven barked a sharp laugh. "I mean, what do you propose?"

Heat creeped up the back of his neck. Language gaffs were an awkward thing, and he always strived to be clear so as to avoid such situations. If he was careful now, she might not realize the level of his embarrassment.

He breathed out a protracted breath. "You may go, *if* you give me your word not to mention tonight's disgraceful conduct of my bodyguard."

Fyad stiffened his stance but blessedly said nothing. Even Elder Kai had taken a few steps back. Was he trying to remove himself from the situation entirely?

"Hmm." Raven seemed to ponder the offer, then shook her head. "Uh-uh. Not good enough."

The corner of his mouth twitched. "What, Ms. Crawford, *would* be good enough?"

She grinned in a way that lifted his nape-feathers. "I want the exclusive story of the trade negotiations."

That was unexpected.

Fyad folded his arms over his chest. "Why? So you can invent lies about that too?"

"No." Raven stomped her foot. "A *real* story."

Fyad barked a harsh laugh. "Your disgraceful employer will never buy it."

"But a legit media outlet might."

She had a point. The beginnings of an idea took shape in Rol's mind. It involved trusting the little human female, though she had yet to prove herself deserving of that honor.

"Ms. Crawford." He paused until she met his gaze. "Let us begin with something simple: an interview."

Interest sparked in her green eyes. "With you?"

With him? The prime advisor to the monarchs of the Raptorclaw clan? The most untouchable of the untouchable advisors? No one had ever dared presume they were so worthy.

"That is not possible, I am afraid. However, you may have an interview with Fyad, my monarchs' bodyguard."

"I'd rather talk to you."

"Consider this a test."

She scoffed. "Because you don't trust me."

Of course, he did not. But he was not confirming that for her. Negotiations were his forte, an artform in their complexity at times. It was how he had convinced the Bezchian Intergalactic Trade Guild to move forward with its dealings with Earth.

I did that to get Captain Shova's Earthling mate off my wings.

For a human, Ava Raptorclaw was a force of nature, particularly when she wanted something. And, for some inexplicable reason, she wanted cinnamon. An Earth spice similar to the sacred Bezchian spice called *cinbin*.

Humans are strange.

He stepped to one side to offer Raven a tantalizing glimpse of freedom. "You could remain here until I have completed my business and returned to my home world."

To say she seemed unhappy about his condition was an understatement, but that was the best he could do for her. And since she could not be trusted, it would have to be enough.

"Prime Advisor," Fyad said. "Would you give us a moment?"

Rol gave the young male a pointed look. "I am not sure that is wise."

"I know, but I think we are both calmer now."

Raven narrowed her suspicion-filled eyes at Fyad but did not argue.

"Very well, then. You have two minutes" He turned to Kai. "Come, Elder."

"I believe I shall retire for the night, Prime."

He studied the older male. Kai still did not appear well. "Is it your time?"

Kai sighed and shook his head as though weary. "No, it is not yet my time. I have never rebirthed before one hundred sun migrations."

The elder turned and shuffled away down the hallway, then disappeared into his room. Well, that was one potential problem put to roost for the night. He moved back to the common area. There was enough to worry about as it was, like what to do about Meryl Faulkner.

Again, with Meryl?

Why did she keep slipping into his thoughts?

The Silverstar Agency had done a great service for Kyzel and Robyn, but something went askew because two more unlikely beings as he and Meryl should not have been matched. Yet, there was something appealing about her. When she was not glaring at him like she would happily pluck all the feathers from his wings.

Footsteps approached and he raised his head. Fyad and Raven entered the space.

39

"We have an agreement," Fyad announced. "She will interview me on Wednesday."

Raven raised both her thumbs in the manner humans did when they deemed things to be positive. "Good to go, your lordship."

"Prime Advisor is acceptable."

"Gotcha." She waved one hand as she sashayed toward the entrance doors. "My ride's waiting. See ya."

The moment the main doors slid shut, Rol turned toward Fyad. The male's gaze was transfixed on the doors even though Raven was gone. Ah, mercy, the infatuation was real—at least, on his guard's part. Yet another thing to keep an eye on.

"Fyad." The way the young male jumped to attention would have been amusing under different circumstances. "You abducted a human female in sight of other humans today. Do you have any idea the trouble that could bring for us? For Bezchi? Explain yourself."

Fyad undid the clasp of the satchel attached to his flying leathers with deft fingers, and pulled out what appeared to be a rolled-up Earth publication called a *magazine*. Why humans still insisted upon using paper for their reading material was beyond him. Fyad opened it, the crinkling of the glossy pages filling the silence, and placed it on the table.

"Here." The guard pointed to the printed bold lettering.

Rol gazed down at it until the verbal translator implant revealed the words: *Bezchian Monarch Tops Lover's Ex.*

He let his gaze track down to the photograph...Kevin Donahue—Robyn's ex-mate—in a tree, staring fearfully up at Kyzel hovering in the air above him. Unfortunately, the article made Kyzel appear as a tyrant, and said nothing about how Donahue had abducted Robyn.

A groan escaped Rol before he could stop it. Yet another problem he did not need.

SIX

Meryl dug the plastic scoop into the ice tray, then tipped it into the heavy glass pitcher. The tinkle of the cubes bouncing merrily off the glass filled her kitchen. It was weird how the sound lifted her spirits. Or maybe it was because Kathy would arrive soon for a visit.

She placed the pitcher on the counter and unscrewed the cap of the limeade bottle. The splash of the liquid brought a smile to her face. Summer might be over, but fall days in SoCal were too warm to tell. All in all, it was a perfect afternoon to sit on the porch sipping with her goddaughter.

"Auntie Meryl, I'm here!"

"Hey, Kit-Kat. I'm in the kitchen."

Kathy strode in, her long, blonde ponytail bouncing from side-to-side and a sparkle in her blue eyes. The perfect twenty-seven-year-old duplicate of Robyn. A pang of nostalgia twisted Meryl's gut. God, did she ever miss her best friend.

But the melancholy could wait. She opened her arms and wrapped the daughter of her heart in a hug. "Missed you."

"Missed you too." Kathy pulled back. "I brought Mom's toasted cheese bites. Can't promise they'll taste as good as hers, but...."

"I'm sure they'll be even better."

Kathy grinned. "I'll grab the tray and help you take everything out. Then you're gonna tell me all about your date yesterday."

Geez, just the little reminder of Rol was enough to send her heart into overdrive. She didn't *want* to be attracted to him, but apparently that didn't matter to her stubborn libido.

A few minutes later, she was comfortably ensconced in one of the brown wicker chairs on her porch, a cool glass of limeade in hand.

"So." Kathy grinned like an imp. "What happened?"

"I don't want to talk about it." Not that that would stop Kat from demanding all the details.

"What? Auntie, you can't leave me hanging. Tell me. Was he cute? Does he look human, or reptilian, or what?"

"*Reptilian*?" She gave her goddaughter a shocked look. "Where'd you get that idea?"

Kat raised her fine blonde eyebrows. "I don't hear you answering."

Touché. Meryl raised her glass to her lips and reveled in a deep sip of the refreshing sweet-tart beverage. Kat was tenacious, and wouldn't let up until she'd learned every gory detail of yesterday afternoon's fiasco. There was no choice but to cave in.

"Fine." She lowered her glass to rest on her lap. "If you must know, my *match* was our friend Rol Raptorclaw."

Kat jerked upright in her rocker. "Get the fuck out. Really?"

"Watch your mouth, child. And yes, really."

If her goddaughter didn't blink soon, the girl's eyeballs might pop out.

Kat blinked, then laughed. And laughed. And doubled over in her chair and laughed even harder, the sound of her amusement filling the yard.

"Well." She sniffed and plucked a cheese toasty from the platter. "Glad *someone* finds this so amusing."

The young woman swiped the back of her hand under one eye and reined in her laughter. "Sorry, Auntie, but you gotta admit, that's like divine retribution."

On so many levels. She popped the savory snack into her mouth and chewed and swallowed. "It sure is. But I think Rol realized how ridiculous it is too, so we're not going out again."

"Did he agree to that?"

"It was a tacit understanding." She ran the pad of her finger around the rim of the glass.

"But, did he *say* it?"

Oh, this girl should've been a lawyer. "Not verbally."

"Ah, ha." Kat looked every ounce of smug. "And I bet *you* didn't say it either."

"Do you even know what the word tacit means?"

Smug gave way to affronted. "Of course I do. And do you know what happens when you *assume* something?"

A snort escaped her. "Smart-ass."

Kat nodded. "I had a great teacher in smart-assery. Maybe you know her?"

"Argh. What happened to that sweet little girl I once knew? She'd never throw my words back in my face." She reached for another toasty. "By the way, these are excellent. I'm suddenly not so worried about your mom being gone."

"Thank you." Kat snagged her own toasty. "So, when are you going to see him again?"

"Do you ever give up?"

Kat grinned evilly. "Like I said, I learned from the best."

There was no denying that fact. She lowered her gaze to the glass so her god-daughter couldn't see how hard she was fighting a smile.

"Kit-Kat, I'm really sorry for getting you involved with my little revenge plot against Rol. I never should've done that to you."

The creak of wicker seemed loud in the silence, then Kat's hand rested on her forearm. "It's okay, Auntie. I'm a big girl now and I knew what I was getting into. I'm actually glad the two of you were matched. He's kinda cute, for an old guy. And I've even forgiven him for what he did to Mom and Kyzel. He did it because he thought it was right."

"You think so?" She peered up and met Kat's gaze.

"Yeah. Besides, he made it up to them in the end by getting Mom out to the galactic spaceport before Kyzel left." She chuckled. "*And*, Rol's action got Dad slapped with a restraining order. So, all's well that ends well, right?"

Well, there was that. She blew out a sigh and Kat withdrew her hand and leaned back in her chair. That evil grin was back, of course. The girl was too smart for her own good. "All right, fine. Yes, I'm going to see him again, *but*…not for a date."

"Why, then?"

"Because, he has a deep-space communicator."

The sharp intake of breath from Kat was audible, probably even to the neighbors. "To talk to Mom?"

"Mm-hmm." She took another sip of her limeade.

"*Eeeee!*" Kat practically bounced in her seat, just like she did when she was a little girl. "When?"

For someone so close to her mother, the last few days must've felt like an eternity. It certainly had for Meryl, and Robyn wasn't even her blood relation.

"After Karen and Kev arrive on Friday." She set her glass on the table between them.

"Thanks, Auntie." The smug look was back. "See? He's not so bad."

A bark of laughter escaped her. "Better than your Uncle Nathan, I guess."

Kat's stricken expression caught her full attention.

"What is it?"

"Nothing." Kat shifted her gaze to the garden as if the camellia bush had suddenly burst into flames.

"Nice try, but no sale. What did Nathan do now?" About the worst thing would be that he'd divorced Charlotte for another woman. Just the thought was enough to give her a mild twinge of sympathy for the little homewrecker.

A very, very mild twinge.

Kat scrunched up her face as if about to deliver bad news. "Charlotte's, um, pregnant."

Her stomach took a nose-dive to her feet, then jammed itself into her throat. God...if he even existed, because at this point that seemed unlikely...had gone and given her ex-husband and that floosy the one thing he'd never given her: a baby.

"Auntie?"

She snapped her attention back to her goddaughter. "Are you sure?"

"Yeah." Kat nodded. "Charlotte told me. She says they've been trying for...um, never mind."

Well, fuck. How novel. Nathan the consummate liar had actually told her the truth that day when she'd caught them in bed.

"A man reaches a certain age when he realizes the importance of progeny. Charlotte can give me that."

Kat leaned forward. "Are you okay, Auntie? What can I do?"

"I'm fine." Sort of. Not really, but Kat didn't need to know. That old, familiar pinpoint of white-hot rage flared in her gut. So much for being over the whole *life's unfair* stage. "Let's change the subject. What's happening at work? Any guys I need to meet with a shotgun?"

Kat's small laugh eased some of the need to throw sharp objects. "You know, you're a scary woman sometimes, Auntie."

SEVEN

Rol rapped his knuckle against the white wooden frame of Meryl's screen door, then took a step back. If he had learned one thing from his friend Kyzel's experiences, it was that Earth females tended to be wary when big, winged males showed up at their front doors in the evenings. Even though Meryl already knew him, it was best to err on the side of caution.

"Just a sec." Her words carried from somewhere deeper in the nest...*house*.

It was strange indeed the way the low timbre of her voice sent a pleasant shiver down his spine.

"Oh." And her breathless gasp the same.

He focused his gaze on the tall, lean, feminine silhouette beyond the screen. If he used his hunting vision, he would be able to see her clear as though nothing stood between them. As it was, though, her shadowy form was enough to appeal to his most masculine senses.

She stepped closer to the door and the details of her features became visible. Her gaze dipped to his flying leathers, then back up. "Um, hi."

Funny how he had never felt exposed when wearing his leather flying straps before. Just the thought of her appreciating his body had him fighting the urge to preen.

Instead, he gave her a nod of respect. "Hello, Meryl."

"W-what are you doing here?"

That was not the greeting he had hoped for, but at least she had not slammed the front door in his face. "I thought you might appreciate a follow-up on yesterday's incident."

"Oh, right." She pushed the screen door open and slid a small piece of metal along the hinge mechanism. "Come on in."

Getting through a narrow, single-person doorway on this planet was always a challenge for beings with wings. But, not impossible, thanks to having watched Kyzel enter Robyn's home. It involved entering with one wing, followed by the body, and finally the second wing. Some head ducking was also required, and all of it would be easier to do if he were younger and more flexible.

He turned sideways, unfurled one wing and contorted his way through until he stood in Meryl's living room.

She raised one corner of her mouth in a smirk, then moved to close the screen door again. "That's pretty impressive, you know."

"I am in awe of myself." He settled his feathers back into place with a quick shake before pulling his wings tighter against his back.

Meryl scoffed. "Of course you are." She waved her hand in the direction of the tall low-backed stools at the raised counter. "Have a seat…a perch, I mean. That's what you call it, right? A perch?"

"Yes." Could she be more aware of his culture than he had credited her? "But seat or stool also work."

"Want something to drink?" She rounded the end of the counter as he slid onto the perch, his long primary feathers brushed over the wood floor. "I picked up some hard cider when I was at the store this afternoon."

He eyed the half-full wine glass on the counter. "One would be nice." Unusually nice, especially after his flight over. "Do you enjoy this beverage too?"

"Nope." She yanked the refrigerator door open with enough force to rattle some glass-encased items together. "I usually prefer wine."

Hence the glass already present. Had she purchased the cider for him, then? He should not be so presumptuous; it could be for another. His gaze was drawn to her backside as she bent and reached into the refrigerator. Her stretchy purple pants adhered to her subtle curves like a lover.

A burning tightness banded across his chest and he curled his fingers into fists. *Is there another?* And who was he to ask such a question, especially when there was no future for them as a mated pair?

"I'm not sure why I even bought it." Meryl straightened and turned, her delicate eyebrows arched high. "But I guess it was a good thing I did, huh?"

He forced his hands to relax and gave her a small smile. "Most fortunate. Thank you. Will you join me with your wine?"

She snapped the cap off the cider bottle and set it on the counter in front of him. "Sure. Why not?"

Why not, indeed?

She settled on the stool next to him, close enough for her unique scent to surround him. Then she raised her glass of deep red liquid. "Cheers."

"Cheers." He tapped his bottle against her glass.

Toasting was an endearing human custom, and one he had never heard of until he came to this planet. It would be something he would miss once he returned home. He pressed the thick rim of the bottle to his mouth and took a deep swallow. Cider too, he would definitely miss that. Maybe he should speak with one of the Bezchian trade delegates and make sure the import of this particular type of alcoholic beverage was on their list of approved items.

He lowered the bottle and sighed at the deep satisfaction the cider brought. Now which of the five representatives would be the most receptive to that suggestion? He was most familiar with Careene's brother, Chiraz, but there was the whole thing about their flock not being consulted first about Kyzel taking a new mate. Perhaps Repeta Rockdweller or Nodi Landwalker would be better choices.

He shifted his gaze to meet Meryl's. Why was she still holding her wine glass up as if they had not already toasted?

She blinked and averted her gaze, her cheeks darkening, then took an exaggerated gulp of her wine. He frowned. She had been staring at him, but why?

"So," she said. "Did you find your guard, and the girl he abducted off the beach?"

He lowered his bottle to the counter. "After searching until well after dark, I returned to the suite to find them both there."

"You're kidding."

"I wish I was."

"Were they making some sort of weird hook-up?"

He gave his head a shake. "What does 'weird hook-up' mean, please?"

"Sometimes, people like to role-play sexual fantasies." She moved her gaze to her glass in her hand, then took another gulp.

She seemed uncomfortable with the topic, but the concept was most intriguing. "No, nothing like that, thankfully. The female was Raven Crawford, the reporter from the publication of questionable ethics."

That caught her attention. "Oh, you mean the one from *Blast off!* who helped us find Robyn after Kevin kidnapped her?"

As if that was enough to redeem the young female. "Yes."

"So, are they interested in each other?" The hint of suggestion sparkled in Meryl's eyes.

It had seemed that way last night, though he hoped he was wrong. Not that his opinion mattered in their case.

"It would never work between them." He focused his gaze on the bottle, turning it a quarter turn at a time atop the counter. "Upon our return to Bezchi, Fyad will submit to the elders for a mate-match. He is thirty-three sun migrations, well past time he provided heirs for our clan."

The soft intake of breath drew his attention back to Meryl. Her normal posture had always been straight, but not like it was now. And the expression in her soulful eyes...was that pain?

"Meryl? What is wrong?"

Those soulful eyes blinked, then cleared as though

returning from a private mental journey. She lowered her gaze to the countertop. "It's nothing."

Her statement did not match the tightness in the line of her jaw, or the heavy clunk as she set her glass on the counter.

"It is *something*." Although, why he suddenly cared enough to pursue it was odd. As odd as the hooded look she was giving him.

Somewhere, an internal voice urged him to run, but his body refused to obey. Instead, his shaft stirred even as the rest of him remained frozen in place. This was an unexpected, yet pleasant development.

Meryl moved like a viper striking. She closed her fingers around his leather flying straps and hauled him toward her. For one who reminded him of Earth's graceful willow tree, her display of physical strength was astonishing. He grabbed the edge of counter with one hand, and the low, metal back of her stool with the other. Then she mashed her mouth to his, her full lips soft yet demanding.

An electric jolt rocketed through him, down to his toes, fingers, the tips of every last wing feather. And he had not been so achingly hard since he was an untried fledgling. He should be questioning…something, but how could he think with a female like his Meryl licking at the seam of his mouth?

He opened to her, drawing her tongue in. The flavor of her wine mingled with the aftertaste of the cider, tangy and satisfying. More, he craved more. Everything she could give, and everything he could give back. He slid off the perch and drew her flush against him.

Every gentle curve of hers was a promise, a gift. The piece of his life he had so patiently waited for, and never believed he deserved. Her moan became his, and the way she rubbed against him was a language he understood even without a translator.

She withdrew, just barely. "I want this, Rol. I *need* this…need *you*."

The torch was lit and set to the kindling. This would happen, and there was no reason to stop. Or, if there was, he could not care less. He fumbled with the cords of his leggings and removed them as Meryl drew off her shirt, pants, and undergarments.

Great skies, she was every bit the long-limbed, graceful creature he had imagined. Her dusky skin, dark nipples, a small, barely visible scar low on her abdomen, a thatch of dark curls at the juncture of her legs instead of a mat of fine, silky feathers.

That was all he saw before she was back, pressed against him. He had not had enough time to remove his flying leathers, but it did not seem to matter. His universe imploded, narrowing down to the two of them. To her, and his consuming need to touch her, taste her, dive deep inside her.

Then they were on the living room rug, her body under his as he moved, kissing her cheek and along her neck to the curve of her shoulder.

"Meryl." Her name came out like a growl, full of need and rightness.

He cupped his hand over one small breast—not so different from a Bezchian female's, but perfect because it was hers. He swirled his tongue around the puckered nub of the other, then sucked it into his mouth hard.

"God, Rol." She pushed her hips against him. "Now...please."

How could he deny her when all he wanted was to feel her around him? There'd be time for slow later, but by the immortals, the fire burning through his very veins would consume him—*them*—if he did not give her what she desired.

He aligned his tip to her opening and thrust his hips forward, driving into Meryl's welcoming heat. Someone cried out in triumph, or maybe they both did. It did not matter as the fire within became an inferno as he pulled almost all the way out and rammed back in.

"Harder," Meryl ordered. "*Harder.*"

Anything she wanted, and any way she wanted it, was his pleasure. He ramped up his rhythm, in and out, in and out, his ridge rings pulsing as he pounded into her over and over. She writhed beneath him, meeting him with an eagerness that matched his own. Then she came with a scream that toppled him over the edge. He buried himself to the base and stiffened, his wings unfurling fully and forcefully as he poured himself into her. Stars exploded behind his eyes, brilliant and beautiful, and seemingly without end.

But they did finally end, winking out one by one as he relaxed his wings, one extended across the floor, the tips of its feathers touching the screen door. The other rested awkwardly over the long, low table in front of her couch, a subtle pain at the *alula* hinting that he had rammed the wing against something. At worst, it would bruise.

All he could focus on was how deliciously soft Meryl was around him, how warm her cheek was against his, and how the sound of their panting in the aftermath eclipsed even the crickets' evening song. For once in his life, everything seemed blessedly right.

He nuzzled his lips against her ear. Words had never escaped him before, but what did one say to top the electrifying union they had just shared? Perhaps words were not necessary.

Meryl moved her hands between them and gave him a little push in the chest. "Get off."

What? Oh, of course. It could not be comfortable to have his greater weight pushing her down against the floor. Even though the rug was thick, there was hardwood underneath.

He used his arms to lever himself up, slipping from her channel with a soft wet sound. Then sat back on his heels between her raised knees. Sweet summer currents, despite her somewhat stunned expression, she all but glowed.

He gave her a grin. "That—"

"You need to leave."

—was…unexpected. "Leave? As in leave your nest?"

"Yes." She scooted away from him, sliding her bottom over the rug. "Get out."

"You cannot possibly—umph." *She threw my leggings in my face.* His reflexes kicked in and he grabbed the article of clothing before it hit the floor. "Why?"

"Because, I said so." She moved around the room, grabbing each article of her clothing, and not looking at him.

"Meryl—"

"I don't owe you an explanation!" She clutched her

bundle to her breasts, her body partially bent as though curling to protect herself from an invisible assailant. "Just leave. Please."

It made no sense. "If that is what you wish."

"I do."

He glowered at her. "Fine."

He bent and stuck one foot through a leg opening, repeated it with the other, then retied the laces. Another round of body and wing contortions, and he was standing on her porch, the cool evening air closing around him. He certainly heard the crickets now.

What just happened?

He had experienced the rawest sex of his life, only to be kicked out moments later. Was this a common reaction for human females?

I do not recall Robyn doing this to Kyzel.

Maybe he should ask Meryl—

Bang!

—or not. The slamming of the front door just reinforced her edict. It was time for him to go, answerless, and his body still humming from the pleasure of her touch.

What the fuck had she been thinking? Revenge sex against her ex with *Rol*, of all people? And with the front door wide open. Talk about taking things too far. The whole neighborhood probably heard her scream.

And scream.

And scream.

Oh. My. God. She couldn't even blame her poor decision-making on the wine. She hadn't had *that* much. She gave the almost empty bottle on the counter a guilty glance. Okay, yes, she'd had *a couple* of glasses before he'd shown up at her door. But only because she hadn't expected anyone to stop by this evening.

Holy Jesus, Mary, and Joseph, the man could screw. And that fluttering sensation inside, whoa. Next time, she was going to take a closer look at that dick of his.

No. There isn't going to be a next time.

She hurried down the hallway to the bathroom. No matter how she felt about Nathan's past transgressions, common sense should've kicked in after that first kiss. But when her entire body had ignited to the temperature of the sun, there'd been no stopping that freight train.

What sixty-three-year-old woman did that? *Without* protection?

She tossed her shirt and yoga pants into the hamper, then reached inside the shower-tub and flipped the handle up. The sound of the water flowing filled the little room.

Girl, you're an educated woman who acted like a college co-ed with a case of the hornies.

The movement of her reflection in the sink mirror caught her attention. People had always told her she looked younger than she was, and maybe that was true, but today she felt older. Hell, with the dark smudges under her eyes and the slump of her shoulders, she *looked* older.

She lowered her gaze and ran her fingers across her abdomen, over the decades old scar, a reminder that love wasn't forever. Nathan should've left her after the surgery.

There had been plenty of other *Charlottes*, as she'd discovered later.

How many times had she seen the exact same scenario played out with clients during her thirty-five years as a divorce lawyer? Hot tear tracks rolled over her cheeks. Men couldn't be trusted. Ever.

The musky scent of Rol's recent lovemaking drifted up. Was it fair to lump him into that group? Yes, yes it was. He was male, and eventually his eye would be caught by some young beauty, probably one with gossamer fairy wings. Why he hadn't already found one was beside the point.

Enough of this little pity party, Meryl Faulkner.

She stepped into the shower and let the hot water cascade over her, washing away the pain of the past, but not the memory of the way Rol had filled her.

EIGHT

———————————— ✦ ————————————

How had everything spun out of control so quickly? Rol turned and paced back across the suite's quiet common area. First, Meryl had flushed him from her nest last night. Then, when he had returned to the suite, he had discovered Elder Kai and Fyad were gone. Disappeared, without a trail of feathers for him to follow.

Although, Fyad had left a scrawled note sitting on top of a back issue of *Blast off!* spread open on the tabletop.

"Prime Advisor, Elder Kai insisted on going on a fly-about. Per your suggestion, I have gone with him. No idea when we will return. Fyad."

All perfectly reasonable, as he *had* told the guard to keep an eye on the old bird. But they *should* be back by now. Correction, *before* now. As in, last night.

How am I going to explain this to Kyzel?

He could not. He must figure out what had become of them and get them back here, post haste, or…. Or what? If he had a clue where to begin a search, that would be something. But, he did not. He must trust in Fyad's ability to

WING AND A PRAYER

handle a verity of situations. That was why he had been selected to accompany Kyzel to Earth in the first place. And why Kyzel had left him here. If the situation turned desperate, the young guard would seek him out.

He breathed out a sigh and shook his wings to release some of the tension through his shoulders. That was better. He had his own priorities to focus on. The preliminary trade negotiations, which would start in a couple of hours—

Bang, bang, bang!

"Now what?" He turned to glare at the door, willing the being on the other side to go away.

Bang, bang, bang!

No such luck.

"Visitor identification." He murmured the words, and the small screen the right of the door lit up to reveal the hallway outside.

It was a female, an Earthling. But not Meryl. He pushed back against the bite of disappointment, and focused on his visitor's petite stature and short-cropped black hair. It could only be Raven Crawford. And why not? Because what he needed right now, more than anything, was another problem.

He cast his gaze upward in a silent plea for mercy. "Door open."

The double sliding doors parted with a faint hiss to reveal his visitor.

Ms. Crawford raised her chin, and something akin to mutiny flashed in her green eyes. "Where is he?"

"Who?"

"That *lying-ass* crow."

Crow? A large black bird of Earth…oh, of course. "You mean Fyad? I have no idea."

"Whaddya mean you have no idea?" She leaned to peer around him. "You're his boss, aren't you?"

Apparently not in the way she defined boss. He stepped to one side and waved her in. "You are welcome to search the premises for him, if you would like."

She did, naturally. Stormed straight through the common room and into the hallway. Humans were a suspicious flock.

He slid onto one of the stools to wait, turning over Fyad's copy of *Blast off!* to peruse. It was full of all sorts of outrageousness, including a bit of nonsense that the Bezchian Intergalactic Trade Guild's list of products to export from Earth included females. Why would anyone on Bezchi want a wingless human female when there were plenty of females—

"Well, he's not there." Raven climbed up on the stool across the table from him and huffed.

He fixed her with a pointed look. "As I said."

"And you don't know where he is?"

"With Elder Kai, somewhere." He shrugged his shoulders. "He will contact me when he is able."

Raven made a sound of doubt. "He said I could interview him this morning, that he'd meet me at the park. I waited *two hours*."

Ah, that explained her pique. "I am very sorry, Ms. Crawford. I am certain he will—how do you say?—make it up to you."

"I don't suppose you'd give me an interview instead? I do have a deadline." Her thin black eyebrows rose halfway to her hairline. How had he never noticed that they seemed to be drawn in, not actual hair like Meryl's?

"The prime advisors of any monarchs never give interviews." He pursed his lips. This might be an ideal opportunity to test her sincerity. "Last time you were here, you suggested you were interested in an exclusive story from inside the trade negotiations. Is this still the case?"

"You bet it is." Her eyes filled with hope.

"I might be convinced to give you the opportunity." He raised one finger before she could respond. "However, there is a stipulation."

"What?"

"You will represent the interests of the *Raptorclaw clan*, not your current employer."

"You mean, I'd be moonlighting for you?"

His translator defined moonlighting as working a second job, which was an acceptable term. "Indeed. But your words must be honorable and true, with no slander toward my clan or anyone else on the negotiation committee. You will get one chance only, Ms. Crawford. I, for one, would like to have your creative talents representing us."

She had no idea this test of her character and abilities was for a more prestigious position in the future. Eventually, the clan would benefit from an Earthling media consultant to advise them. A spokesperson of sorts.

Despite the questionable ethics of her current employer, Raven Crawford seemed savvy in her field, and he did sense a foundation of trustworthiness within her that was not being utilized through her current job. If he could earn her loyalty now, so much the better.

"Wow." She grinned as if he had handed her a jar of the most sacred *cinbin* spice. "I'd really like that, sir."

Ah, sincerity. Finally. "Excellent. Because the preliminary trade negotiations start this afternoon."

Her mouth popped open and her eyes widened. "But the representatives weren't supposed to be back in L.A. until tomorrow."

He gave her a conspiratorial grin. "Good thing you stopped by here today, then. Shall we go?"

Earth's Intergalactic Relations and Commerce buildings rose like twin silver knife-blades in Los Angeles's skyline. They were not the tallest buildings, but they were by far the most futuristic, at least in comparison to their neighbors. The interior hallways, offices, and session rooms were built wide to accommodate a plethora of sizes and shapes—much like the Silverstar building. They also had convenient, and not overly used, rooftop access.

Not so convenient, though, was the security checkpoint just inside the roof atrium lobby. On Bezchi, Rol was recognized, but on Earth....

He waved his wrist over the identification scanner. Next to him, Raven tugged her credentials out of her black camera bag.

The female security guard watching the monitor blinked. "*Oh*. Prime Advisor Raptorclaw, we didn't expect you."

"I sent a message that I would arrive with a guest within the hour."

"I'm sorry." The guard tapped the keys of her keyboard.

"Let me get your clearance verified."

He inclined his head. "Of course."

Raven leaned close to him. "I'm gonna get one of those wrist implants once they're available."

"They are not available on Earth yet?" How could that be? Earth had joined the Galactic Alliance of Planets over ten sun migrations ago.

"Oh, they're available, *if* you're important enough. But I'm not rich or a world leader, so I get to wait."

He frowned down at her. "They should be available to all."

"Ya think?" She shrugged her hands and her shoulders.

"Yes, I do." It was an Alliance law, surely.

The security female looked up. "You are cleared, Prime Advisor. May I see your ID, ma'am?"

Raven handed over her card and the female scanned it. "You're with...*Blast off!*?" She squished up her nose and looked at Rol as if there was some mistake.

"She is with the Raptorclaw clan, retained by *me* as a media liaison." He reached across the counter and plucked the card from between her fingers. "We are attending the preliminary trade negotiations this afternoon."

"Oh." The security female still seemed uncertain, her gaze flitting back and forth between him and Raven.

Enough of this. "Come along, Ms. Crawford."

He handed her identification back to her and strode into the building.

The muffled thump of Ms. Crawford's thick-soled boots against the acoustic flooring followed him, until she trotted at his side. "Thanks for that."

"For what?"

"People don't usually stand up for me." She hitched her camera bag higher on her shoulder.

"That is where you are wrong."

"Pretty sure I'm not. Could you slow down a little?"

He stopped and faced her. "It is your employer others are unwilling to stand up for, not you, Ms. Crawford. You would do well to remember that."

"I'd quit today, but can't afford to."

And nor should she. If she proved herself unworthy of the position with the clan, she would at least have employment to fall back on. No matter what happened, he would not leave anyone without the means to survive.

"Honor is one of the few things in life a being can truly call their own." He allowed a small smile. "Would you not agree, Ms. Crawford?"

She opened her mouth, then snapped it shut again and nodded.

The youngling was trying. "Patience, Ms. Crawford. If necessary, I will see to your *temporary* credentials for the duration of the trade negotiations."

She returned his smile. "I understand, and I won't let you down."

"I expect no less. Now, be warned, today's proceedings will not be…exciting. It will be a review of all the places the representatives visited, followed by a dinner."

"A dinner?" She glanced down at her less-than-suitable attire.

"We will not stay for that." He gestured down the hallway with one hand. "Shall we try to figure out where the session will be held?"

It took them less time than he had anticipated to locate the venue: Session Room Twelve on the forty-ninth floor—two floors down from the roof, presumably for easy access for the Bezchian representatives and their staff.

The wide double door whisked open for him with the barest whisper, and he stepped into the room. It was large enough to accommodate a mid-sized flock of Bezchians and their wings. Plus an equal number of humans.

A chest-high circular table surrounded by a dozen cushioned stools dominated the center of the room. Half of those stools had no backs, making them ideal for use by the Bezchian trade delegates. Spaced evenly around the room's perimeter were observation perches of both the Bezchian and human variety.

At the far end of the table, five Bezchians gathered in a loose circle. The representatives of the trade guild, one from each clan: Raptorclaw, Landwalker, Rockdweller, Water-diver, and Firewing.

"Wow," Ms. Crawford breathed. "What a view, huh?"

It was indeed. Beyond the floor-to-ceiling windows, were the city, suburbs, and distant mountains that separated the oceanside dwellers from the sparsely populated desert region, where the spaceport was located.

He turned from the magnificent panorama and flicked his fingers in the direction of the observation seats. "You and I will sit with the staff members."

"Okay." Ms. Crawford nodded.

"But first, introductions." He strode toward the gathered group, and Raven hurried to keep up.

Sharla Waterdiver met his gaze and her expression

brightened. "Prime Advisor Raptorclaw, how good it is to see you here."

"Likewise, Representative Waterdiver." He gave her a nod of respect. "This is Ms. Raven Crawford, a reporter, here to observe the proceedings as my guest."

Sharla inclined her brown and tan feathered head at Raven. "Delighted to meet you, Ms. Crawford. These are Representatives Nodi Landwalker, Repeta Rockdweller, Odu Firewing, and Chiraz Raptorclaw."

The other two females and two males murmured greetings.

"How was your global tour of Earth?" Rol met Chiraz's gaze.

Chiraz raised his chin a fraction. "Insightful, Prime Advisor."

There was a hint of coolness in his tone. It was possible that, as Careene's brother, he still harbored mild resentment over Rol backing Kyzel's choice to take a human as his new mate.

"Very much so," Sharla agreed. "I, for one, am amazed and thrilled at how the humans have managed solar glass technology. Did you know that all the windows in this building convert sunlight into energy, making it almost completely self-sufficient? And, the glass is fully recyclable."

"So, the rumors are true, then." This was technology worth negotiating for.

Chiraz shook his head. "It is currently only seventy percent efficient, though. If we can get the technology, I am confident we could make it one hundred percent efficient."

"And be penalized by the Alliance for stealing." Sharla raised her brows. "This is their invention, Chiraz, one of the few they came up with before any other planet in the Alliance did."

"My apologies for the delay." A brown-skinned, hairless human male swept into the room, followed closely by three aides. "Our official meeting itinerary for tomorrow is back on track, if you'd all like to take a seat."

The human's voice was deep and strong, and commanded instant respect. Rol grasped Ms. Crawford by the elbow and guided her toward a pair of chairs, one Earthling and one Bezchian.

Once settled, Ms. Crawford leaned toward him. "We were working on solar glass years before the Alliance made contact. Damn right it's *ours*."

NINE

———— ✳ ————

Rol exited the kitchen of the suite, a glass of water in each hand. The preliminary session had closed mid-afternoon without a dissenting word. All the main participants had then retired to their accommodations to prepare for dinner later this evening, which was sure to be attended by many of those Ms. Crawford had referred to as the *upper crust*.

An evening immersed in politics and making connections would have been relaxing. But, it was too soon to trust Ms. Crawford to continue behaving herself. Bringing her back to the Silverstar suite had seemed like the safer option. It was disappointing to find that Fyad and Elder Kai still had not returned, though. Nor had Meryl left a message via the agency. That particularly stung.

He set one glass of water on the dining table in front of Ms. Crawford. "What are your impressions of the session?"

The young human smoothed her hands over her hair, but it did not help tame the wild mess it had become on the flight home. "It was interesting. Insightful." She met his gaze as he claimed the perch across from her. "It's different."

"How so?"

"My focus, I guess." She wrapped her hands around her glass. "I'm not writing about people's...no, that's not right. It's...I don't have to make shit up this time."

"Mm, yes. It is best to stick to the facts." He raised his glass and took a measured swallow.

"Yeah." She huffed. "But I kept catching myself wondering if there's something romantic going on between representatives Rockdweller and Raptorclaw."

The water caught in his throat as a laugh pushed its way out and he ended up coughing.

"You okay?"

"Y-yes." Somehow, he managed to choke out the word.

Imagine that, Repeta and Chiraz as mates? Inconceivable, as clans did not intermingle, except for the Firewings. They had a whole mating process that he still had not figured out, other than they usually waited nearly a thousand sun migrations to find their mates. Must be difficult to be so long-lived.

He coughed once more, cleared his throat, then refocused on the human reporter. "That is not very likely, as Chiraz is already mated and has four heirs."

"So?" Raven shrugged. "When has that stopped a guy?"

"Do not apply Earthling ethics to Bezchians, Ms. Crawford. In the Raptorclaw clan, we mate for life."

How would Meryl feel about that?

Raven raised one eyebrow. "What about other clans?"

"Most of the others do too."

"Which means some don't?"

71

He narrowed his eyes at her. "Is this the story you are looking for?"

"Shit." She slapped her hand over her mouth. "I'm sorry. Years of habit."

"Focus on the primary players and what they bring to the negotiations."

"Right, okay." She picked up her notebook and pen. "Let's start with Chiraz Raptorclaw's experience first, then. What made him qualified to represent your clan?"

Now she was understanding the game. "He started out very young in politics, spent almost two sun migrations as a lesser advisor for Monarch Kyzel's predecessors. He resigned when his older sister, Careene and her mate were elected our new monarchs after the last pair stepped down."

"Wait, his *sister* was Monarch Kyzel's first mate?" She shook her head. "Wow, bad reporter. I had no idea that they were so closely related. What happened to the monarchs before them?"

"They served for sixty-eight sun migrations, until one was afflicted with the mindlessness. They stepped down together, and our people chose Kyzel and Careene as their successors."

"The mindlessness...that's like Alzheimer's, right?"

He shook his head. "I do not know this, but it is a slow deterioration of one's cognizance. Hence the reason the pair stepped aside. It is not possible to rule and care for—"

Tap, tap, tap.

Rol directed a frown at the door. Who could that be?

"Excuse me a moment, Ms. Crawford." He strode toward the door and it opened.

The vision it revealed was nearly enough to stop his heart. "Meryl."

The green-gray button-down shirt she wore brought out the hints of green in her haunted eyes, and the faded jeans gave her legs the illusion of going on for miles. Legs that had been wrapped around his hips just last night.

Take yourself by the wing, Rol.

A smile slid up as natural as a sunrise. "Please, come in."

"I...okay." She stepped through the doorway and the doors slid closed again.

It was a colossal mistake to have shown up at Rol's unannounced like this. Meryl pressed her lips together hard. Seeing him again was, well, it was a damn relief that he hadn't caught the first ship home already, although he might still do that after he heard what she had to say. The need to see him faded into indecision in the reality of his imposing, and incredibly sexy, presence wearing nothing but his flying leathers and tight black pants. Leggings. Whatever they were called didn't change the fact that she knew exactly what was inside them.

Stop it!

How was she going to get through this?

She worried her lower lip between her teeth. "Do you have a minute?"

"Of course. Your timing is perfect. Ms. Crawford was just leaving."

Raven Crawford is here?

"Yep." The young lady in question stepped around Rol, her ever-present camera bag slung over her shoulder, and a notebook in hand. "Leaving now. Nice to see ya, Ms. Faulkner. Thanks for the insight, Rol; I'll check in with an update after tomorrow's session."

A kernel of suspicion wormed into Meryl's heart as Raven bounced out. She had called him by his first name.

Like I have any claim on him.

She'd kicked him out of her house, for crying out loud.

Rol took a step closer. "You wish to speak to me?"

"Um, yeah." She wished to do more than speak, but that wasn't going to happen again. Especially once she told him the truth. "It turns out that I do owe you an explanation for last night after all."

His dark gaze seemed to sharpen, but he shook his head. "You do not owe me anything, Meryl."

If only his tone was harsh instead of understanding, it would make this a little easier. A little less hurtful.

"I do, actually." She lowered her gaze to her clasped hands, then back to his face. "I used you as revenge against my ex last night, and I'm sorry."

Pain flashed in those mysterious eyes, and he raised his chin a fraction of an inch.

She spread her hands in a pathetic silent attempt to plead understanding. "I thought I was beyond being so stupid, but I guess not."

"What did *he* do?" His words came out in a low growl that sent a shiver through her.

There was no way she was going to tell him that, so she

74

gave her head a sharp shake, then swiped a strand of hair from her cheek.

He pressed his lips together in a flat line. "I see."

She swallowed hard and nodded. The silence creeped in like a malicious disease, filling the room with its miasma. As much as she'd hoped her confession would help, the truth was, it was worthless without facts to back it up. Facts that were too personal to share with someone she'd known for such a short time.

Besides, he was a guy, and by definition untrustworthy.

She lowered her gaze, searching for something more forgiving than Rol's hard expression to focus on.

"Well." She made a shrugging motion with her hands. "I guess I'll be going now."

"Good day, Ms. Faulkner."

Ouch. His cold tone cut into her heart, but probably not as much as she'd sliced his. There was nothing left to do but turn around and walk out.

"See ya, Rol." Her whispered words mocked her as she turned and left.

And if her heart ached at the smothering of a fragile hope, it was the least she deserved.

Numbness washed over Rol as Meryl turned and left.

How dare she?

But she *had* dared. She had told him that everything he had been feeling was based on a lie. Her lie. There was no longing in her cold heart for him; he had only been a means to an end. Revenge against the male who she still must have feelings for, even though he was no longer part of her life.

Staying on Earth was a waste of time now. For a short while, he had allowed himself to secretly hope that someone like him could find a mate on this distant planet. He had even dared believe in finding a relationship similar to Kyzel and Robyn's. A rare one of love and trust.

But, it was not to be.

He wadded up the aching sense of loss and shoved it down deep where he would not succumb to its strident emotions. It was time to prepare to return to Bezchi.

He strode to the communication room. "Hail Kyzel."

The deep-space communicator responded to his voice instantaneously, the slim, rectangular box changing from white to blue. A moment later, an image flickered over it before solidifying into a miniature version of a smiling, blonde-haired, blue-eyed Earthling female.

He touched his hand to his heart and bowed. "Kee mohap." My monarch.

"Hey, Rol." Robyn was dressed in black flared leggings of Earth design, and the female version of flying leathers, which must have been custom-made for her. Very few Raptorclaw females were as full-figured.

She was also altogether too animated for his current mood.

"You appear to be settling in well. Is Kyzel present?"

"Nope, he's off doing something official. Can I give him a message?"

"Please. Would you tell him I will be leaving on the next ship to Bezchi?"

She perked up with a grin. "Is Meryl coming too? You know, when you told us you two had been matched, I—"

"No."

"Oh." Her entire body seemed to deflate, and her cheeky smile with it. Then she narrowed her eyes in a calculating manner. "What happened, Rol? If it involves Meryl, you need to tell me."

Where did she get *that* notion? "I do not *need* to tell you."

Monarch or not, his personal life was *his*.

"Okay, then, let me tell *you* something—"

"Please do not—"

"Shut up, dummy. This is important. I know Meryl can be prickly and hard to understand sometimes—"

"Often." Except when she was soft and pliable and writhing under him.

"But you need to know that her ex left her with very little reason to ever trust guys again."

His innards seemed to twist up on themselves. He did not know this about her. "It would help if someone would tell me what happened."

Robyn shook her head. "Not my story to tell. My point is, before you run away with your tail...wings...whatever, between your legs, ask yourself if you have bothered to take the time to understand *why* she is the way she is."

In truth, he had not pursued the topic with his usual prime advisor persuasiveness, so it was possible that Robyn's point was valid.

Robyn's expression softened. "I dunno what happened between you two, but I suspect Meryl did something dumb."

"She used me."

"Ah, yes. Revenge sex." She pursed her lips and drew her eyebrows together. "I was afraid of that. Here's the thing, Rol. She lost her dream a few years ago when her ex-husband left her. She was finally getting her life back together, and then I upped and left her too. Her best friend took off—and for another planet, no less. You gotta imagine that hurts, no matter how supportive she is of me outwardly."

"I can understand that." Did not want to, but he did.

"So, do me one itsy-bitsy favor. Search your heart and see if there's even a tiny chance to work things out. At the very least, don't leave her on bad terms, okay? Please?"

He closed his eyes and breathed out a resigned sigh. To say he did not want to give Meryl another chance was untrue, and to say he was relieved by Robyn's words would be an understatement. It seemed Meryl was a good person who had been hurting for a long time.

He opened his eyes and gave Robyn a nod. "I will try, kee mohap, but not because you asked me to."

Robyn's mouth twitched, curving up into a pleased smile. "That makes me even happier."

TEN

---*---

When everything else in the world seemed to be going wrong, the garden was always there. Here Meryl could lose herself in the peaceful beauty of the outdoors. The happy splash of water from the birdbath fountain, the hum of a bee collecting pollen, the chatter of a squirrel in the neighbor's tree—all of it was nature's orchestra.

She placed the bulb planter on the soil and gave it a push into the soft dirt. It just didn't get much better. And thankfully the latest heatwave was over, although the furnace would turn back on just in time for Karen and Kev's visit this weekend.

The whisper of wings cutting through the air reached her ears, and a shadow moved over her.

Jesus, that's a big bird.

She sat back on her heels, placed her hand on her straw sunhat, and tipped her head back. Nothing. She'd missed it. Probably one of those turkey vultures.

"Behind you."

She drew in a sharp breath and twisted partway around. "Rol?"

It was *him*, the one person she'd never expected to see again. He was standing in her backyard wearing his usual black pants and leather flying straps. And holding a bouquet of—were those roses? They were the loveliest color of apricot.

One side of his mouth quirked up in a crooked smile. "Being that our closest friends are mated, I figured it was best we were on amicable terms at the very least."

"Probably." She worried her bottom lip between her teeth. "But what I did…that was pretty awful."

His smile faded a bit but didn't fully disappear. "Yes, it was. But I came here to talk…like adults."

"Like adults works. I just don't have any fight left in me, to be honest." She pushed herself off the ground and walked toward him as she tugged off her gardening gloves, finger by finger.

His chuckle was warm, not deprecating. "You will never completely run out of fight, Meryl. Here, these are for you."

"A peace offering?" She reached out to accept the roses from him, but it was the faint scent of him that set her heart skipping. The big guy was racking up sweet points, that was for sure.

"Of a sort." He shrugged his shoulders. "They were for you whether you agreed to talk to me or not."

Okay, more sweet points. "I'll put these in water and grab us something to drink. Be right back."

He nodded.

She dropped her gloves on the deck and tugged at the

handle of the heavy sliding glass door. It opened with a rumble and the air-conditioned coolness of her house flowed over her as she stepped inside and slid the door closed.

He wants to talk.

That was a start, at least. She pressed her hand over her heart. More importantly, he didn't seem angry, which meant there was a chance they could do this without degrading into a sparring match. Wouldn't that be a refreshing change?

But how much should she tell him? He wasn't here because he wanted to exchange recipes.

Stop thinking. Just...stop, okay?

She grabbed the tall, white ceramic pitcher off the dining room table and moved toward the kitchen. It'd been hard enough to face him yesterday to tell him the truth, but he'd deserved some sort of explanation. And she really didn't want to end their relationship...such as it was...on a bitter note.

A groan lodged in her throat as she flipped the faucet handle and the soft shush of water filling the pitcher soothed her. Even though her intent had been to work out her personal demons through sex, something had changed the moment she'd kissed him. Something she'd been peripherally aware of at the time but it hadn't hit her until later that night. She *liked* the guy. As in really, really, I-want-to-keep-seeing-you liked him.

Nothing like that had happened since the divorce, and was there anything more terrifying? The last thing she needed was to stick her heart out there again.

She shut off the water and placed the roses in the pitcher. They would look pretty on the patio table. She snagged two bottles from the fridge—hard cider for him, wine spritzer for her—between her fingers and carried the lot back out to the deck.

Outside, Rol had settled himself on the deck bench-railing, looking out over her little backyard with his wings low and relaxed, their long tips fanned over the redwood planks.

He turned partway around, his gaze traveling from her face to the roses and back. "Very lovely."

"Thanks." Wait. Did he mean the flowers, or her?

Nah. Must be the flowers.

She set the pitcher on the cast iron table and turned one of the matching chairs around, careful to avoid setting it on his wing feathers. It seemed a little too intimate to share the bench with him, at least at this point.

He pivoted to straddle the bench, lifting one wing over to the garden side. His closest wing brushed her ankle sending a wave of goosebumps up her leg and straight to her nipples. Dammit.

She extended the cider bottle to him. "Here you go."

"Thank you." He twisted the cap off as naturally as if he'd been doing so for years. "What should we toast to?"

"Um, I don't know." She pressed her palm against the cap of her bottle and gave it a twist. The soft whisper of air releasing seemed so normal, comforting. "How about, new beginnings?"

"How about—" he touched the neck of his bottle to hers with a soft clink of glass. "—honest beginnings?"

She swallowed around the knot in her throat. Talk about setting the bar high. Not that she'd intended to lie, but it was very clear that he wasn't leaving without the whole story.

"Honest beginnings." She brought the bottle to her mouth and tipped her head back. The cold, fruity liquid flowed over her tongue.

Rol took two long swallows, his Adam's apple bobbing— did the Bezchians call it that, or something else?

He lowered the bottle and sighed with pure male satisfaction. "Refreshing after a hot flight over here."

A laugh bubbled out of her before she could stop it, and he grinned as though it was the nicest sound he'd heard all day.

He placed the bottle between his dark-clad thighs. "How about I start?"

"You?" What did *he* have to confess?

"Unless you are not curious as to what inspired me to come over."

"I am now."

"Good." He inhaled deeply then exhaled. "I accidently spoke to Robyn after you left last evening."

"Accidently?"

He shrugged one shoulder. "I called Kyzel, but she answered."

"Okay. Why?"

"Why did I call him?" He paused, and she gave him a nod. "To let him know I was coming home."

Her heart plummeted to her stomach. "Oh."

"But Robyn inspired me to question my decision." He raised his hand to stop her from interrupting. "And she made me promise not to leave without having things settled between us."

Wasn't that just like her friend, always looking out for her, even from lightyears away?

Rol dipped his chin and gave her a look of compassion. "What did he do to you, Meryl, that keeps you from letting me get closer?"

A snort escaped her. "Maybe I just don't want...." No, that was the same defensive attitude that got her into this mess. But, she'd never talked to anyone about this before. Not even Robyn knew every detail. Her friend had had her own shit going down at that time, and it'd always seemed unfair to add to her burden. "Sorry. It's...hard to talk about."

This was it, the part where he threw up his hands and walked out. Or flew off, as the case may be.

Yet he hadn't moved. And damn if that wasn't understanding in his eyes. But why?

"It is all right if you are not ready yet." Rol extended one hand. "Will you sit with me instead?"

There was no reason not to. Besides, her hand was determined to do its own thing anyway, because it was already in his, fully without her permission. In fact, it seemed like her entire body had rebelled against her.

He swung his leg back over the bench and drew her down to sit next to him, facing the yard. Then he smiled, took another swig of his cider, and turned to gaze at the row of rhododendrons along the back fence.

ELEVEN

———————✳———————

Mcryl raised her bottle to her lips, savoring the sweet flavor and mild tang of the wine spritzer. The silence between them, punctuated by an occasional bird chirp, was kind of nice. Two robins flew in to splash in the stone birdbath. Bit by bit, the tension in her shoulders dissipated.

Weird that she couldn't come up with even one memory of a moment as casually intimate as this with Nathan. Sure, there'd been quiet alone times, but this was somehow different. More secure.

Undeniably right.

And what did she have to lose here anyway. Besides Rol's respect, if she'd ever had that.

I must have, or why else would he have come here?

She took another sip, then lowered her bottle to her lap and ran her tongue over her lips. "I was thirty-three when I met Nathan. He was twenty-eight. We worked at the same family law firm. He'd already been there a few years when I came on board. We worked together well, and he was so easy to like."

What hadn't there been to like about him? Tall…taller than her six feet, even…wavy light brown hair and eyes so blue the sky was jealous. He was kind to their clients, but tough with the opposing counsel. Hell, even her parents had liked him.

Rol turned his head toward her, slightly tilted. Even though he said nothing, that little sign of attentiveness bolstered her confidence.

She gave her shoulders a shrug. "When he proposed, it seemed like a no-brainer. When he suggested we open our own law practice, it was another no-brainer." She huffed a derisive laugh. "Then, I was diagnosed with cervical cancer, and ended up having a complete hysterectomy. He told me everything would be fine, that we didn't need children to be a family. And, surprise, surprise, my brain stepped out of the room, again."

She'd believed everything so blindly, like a gullible child. "He was so god*damn* good at hiding the truth."

Every painful lie.

"What truth?" Rol's voice rumbled over her, low and expectant.

The burn of tears stung her eyes and she picked at the label on the bottle with one fingernail. "That I wasn't good enough. I wasn't *enough*, period. He'd been fucking other women our entire marriage."

Rol sat up even straighter than normal, like just the concept of men cheating was offensive. Which was probably the case. Robyn had told her that members of his clan mated for life.

She swiped her knuckles under her eyes, and they came away wet. "Not everybody takes their marriage vows seriously. I found that out the day I walked in on him screwing our new secretary, in *our* bed."

"Meryl...."

"He didn't stop boinking her even though I was there." A harsh laugh escaped her. "It only took a couple more seconds, anyway. Then, he told me he'd only stayed with me out of concern. He made it sound like I would've gone suicidal if he'd left me right after my hysterectomy."

All while that slut Charlotte had tossed her silky dark hair and smiled smugly, like she'd won the most coveted grand prize ever. *As if.*

"I think it was really because I was a better lawyer than him, frankly. Don't know how many times he called me the queen of research after we negotiated a winning deal for a client." She rolled her bottle between her palms, the beverage sloshing with the motion. "But, the worst part was when he told me Charlotte could give him the children I never did."

Rol curled his fingers into fists on his muscular thighs. Was he angry on her behalf?

She gave one giant fist a pat. "Don't worry, big guy. I made sure the divorce settlement came down on my side."

Poor little Charlotte didn't get the three-thousand-square-foot house on the beach...*she* did. And then she'd sold it to some famous, middle-aged, A-list action movie actor and his librarian wife for a pretty sum.

"And that is why you had sex with me?"

"No." She forced herself to meet his gaze. "I did that

because I had just found out that Charlotte is finally pregnant."

Because the dickhead who'd left her questioning the integrity of every man in the universe had got the baby he'd wanted so much. The child she'd never have. And the news had run her heart through the grinder yet again, like it'd been days, not years, since she'd walked in on the two of them going at it. For all her life experiences and degrees and suffixes, she still didn't understand the mysteries of the human brain.

The strength of Rol's hand wrapped around hers, palm to palm, their fingers intwined. "I have your wingside, Meryl."

The ice wall around her heart cracked, giving way to the torrent of pain she'd so carefully packed away behind it. She leaned against him. "He told me everything would be okay, and I believed him."

Hot tears flowed free from her eyes, burning over her cheeks before rolling down Rol's chest. Her breathing turned ragged and her shoulders shook. Years of grief seemed all too eager to break free now, and there was no stopping it.

And this time she didn't try—it needed to come out. Not in dribs and drabs, but in a blubbering, slobbering, cleansing mess. And she gave into it, let it shake her, gut her, tear her soul out.

Eventually, the flood ebbed to a trickle. The hollow cavity in her center filled with a rare peace, and her soul settled back even as an occasional hiccup escaped.

Rol still held her hand and a faint scent hovered around her. That nice, cozy autumn scent of allspice, even though it wasn't officially autumn yet.

She sniffled and raised her head. "I'm sorry. I made a mess of your flying leathers."

"They will dry." Understanding and something deeper, shone in his eyes. Then he handed her a square of cloth. "You may hold this in case you need it again."

A small, watery laugh slipped out and she accepted the hanky. "Thanks." She dabbed it over her cheeks.

"I should thank you." There was so much sincerity in his deep voice.

She paused mid-dab and met his gaze. "Why?"

"It took a lot to trust me with your pain. My heart is full of warmth."

What a lovely thing to say. Now if her brain could come up with some sort of reply. It seemed curiously empty at the moment. And Rol's gaze was so full of reassurance and understanding.

He placed his other hand over their joined ones. "Sometimes, when there is nothing more left to say, the best thing to do is to enjoy the scenery." He nodded his head in the direction of the yard. "Your garden is beautiful."

She couldn't hold back the smile. "Thank you."

There was a flash of satisfaction in his eyes, then he gazed out over her yard, bathed in the shimmering light of the afternoon sun. He was right. Her garden was beautiful. The purples and blues of the rhododendrons were muted, and the night-blooming jasmine scented the air. A soft cooing of a pair of nesting mourning doves singing to their little ones came from under the bougainvillea in the back corner.

It was nice to have someone undemanding to share this quiet moment with, even for a little while. Especially now that her whole body felt lighter than it had in…well, in too damn long. More amazing was that she'd allowed herself to be vulnerable with him. Trusted him with her deepest pain, and he *had her wingside.*

She allowed herself a soft sigh, then rested her head against Rol's shoulder. A faint rustle behind her caught her attention, then the end of his wing appeared as he curved it around her—not touching, but sheltering.

A satisfying warmth spread through her, a sense of rightness because she'd opened up to him and he had not run away. Maybe there was hope.

TWELVE

———◆———

Rol entered the dimly lit suite, the elation from an afternoon and evening spent with Meryl carried him like a Floating Crystal of Pirliv. How it was that things had gone so well between them, only the immortals knew, but he would not question the gift.

After she had unburdened herself of the specter of her past, they had sat together in surprising companionship for nearly an hour. Few words had been spoken because the peaceful beauty of her backyard had been more than enough. Until it was broken by one of her neighbors coming out to start their *char-coal bar-be-que*.

Now that was something new...bar-be-que. Who knew such a genius way of cooking meat existed on this planet? But it did, and Meryl was an expert *bar-be-que-er*.

And she will come by tomorrow with Robyn's entire brood.

It was surprising how he now looked forward to meeting Karen and Kevin, Jr. Nothing like his initial reluctance the day she'd suggested he allow the younglings to come over and use the deep-space communicator.

The memory drew a chuckle from him.

She did out-maneuver me.

He paused in the center of the common room. "Elder Kai?"

No response.

"Fyad?"

Still nothing.

Why had they not returned? And, where could they be?

It was nearly midnight, fast approaching the dawn of day three of their absence. "Lights at full."

The track lighting in the ceiling brightened. Nothing was out of place, so they had not even been back. A brief check-in would have been courteous.

He released a long, slow sigh. There was nothing for it. He must report their absence to Kyzel.

"You *lost* the elder?" Kyzel's voice cracked over the deep-space communicator's speaker, even as surprise flashed in his ice-blue eyes.

Rol cringed at the accusation. "You know how difficult it is to make his kind listen to reason."

And the Firewing clan was notorious for not listening.

Kyzel's wings drooped a bit and he shook his gray-feathered head. "They are indeed a flighty flock."

"I don't get it," Robyn said. "*Why* are they that way?"

"Because," Kyzel's expression softened with his mate. "The Firewing clan focuses most of their energy on matching mates. When they are not doing that, they tend to get distracted by flights of fancy."

"And here I thought A.D.D. was just a human diagnosis," Robyn muttered.

"Fyad is gone too." Rol gave his shoulders a shrug. "His note indicated he went with Kai, as I did ask him to watch him."

Kyzel nodded. "This is good. But if he returns without Elder Kai…"

"I will implement a search."

"Perfect." Kyzel seemed satisfied with this plan. "Anything else?"

"That is all, my monarch."

"Wait," Robyn leaned in closer to the camera. "What about Meryl? Did you two talk?"

Rol allowed himself a half-smile. "Yes. And I will be staying a while longer."

She smiled back and nodded. "I'm glad."

"She and your younglings will be coming over tomorrow to communicate with you, unless you do not wish it?"

Her smile widened. "You bet I wish it!"

"Then it shall be." He inclined his head to both of them. "Good night, my monarchs."

THIRTEEN

———————✴———————

The door to the suite slid open with a soft sigh, like a woman when a gorgeous man walked by.

Meryl laughed internally. *Or like I do with Rol standing there just inside, like he's the lord of the manor.*

She gave the big lug of a bird a grin. "Good morning."

"Good morning, Meryl." The three little words spoken in his deep voice set her insides quaking in the most pleasant way.

She tipped her head in the direction of Robyn's kids. "Karen and Kev's flights were on time, so here we are."

"I see that." Amusement sparkled in his eyes.

"You've met Kathy already."

Kat gave him a little wiggly finger-wave. "Hi again."

"Pleasure to see you again, Ms. Donahue." Rol inclined his head politely.

"Kathy's fine."

"As you wish."

"And," Meryl glanced in the direction of Robyn's other two kids. "This is Karen and Kev."

Kev extended his right hand. "That's what you should call us, too. Not Mr. or Ms. Donahue."

Karen snorted softly but didn't correct her brother. Robyn's oldest daughter had dumped Donahue like yesterday's garbage and embraced Simmons when she'd married Paul three years ago.

Rol clasped Kev's outstretched hand. "Then I shall. Please, come in. Your mother is already waiting on the deep-space communicator."

A faint, allspice-y scent—all Rol—wafted passed her nose. The memory of his big wing curved protectively around her last night jumped to the forefront of her thoughts.

Karen stepped into the common area. "Thank you for letting us come over to talk to her."

Her gaze darted around the room, as though expecting something to jump out at her. Always the protective oldest sibling.

"My pleasure." Rol seemed to be studying each of the kids, probably noting their similarities to Robyn. They all had her blonde hair and sky-blue eyes. "Your mother arrived on Bezchi a few days ago, so the connection will be much clearer than when they were aboard the ship. As she is anxious to speak with you, we should not keep her waiting. This way, please."

Once everyone was settled in the communication room and chatting animatedly with Robyn, Rol made a move toward the door.

So ya think you're sneaking out without me, huh?

She followed him, like steel to his magnet. The door to

the communication room closed behind her with another one of those silly sighs.

Rol fixed her with a quizzical frown. "Do you not wish to speak with your friend?"

"Oh, I will." She gave her shoulders a small shrug. "I figured the kids should have their alone time with her first."

"Ah." He smiled down at her. Had he always had dimples in his cheeks? "They are pleasant younglings, so much like their mother."

A tiny laugh bubbled out. "Karen can be a bit surly at times, but that's because she's protective of Kat and Kev." And Robyn too.

"The nature of the first-born." He nodded knowingly. "I see it with Kyzel's fledglings as well. Would you like something to drink while you wait?"

Her gaze tracked down to his chest. Such a shame those pecs were hidden under his Bezchian-style shirt.

"I could remove my omlek if you like." Rol's low spoken words hit her straight between the legs.

A flame of heat raced to her cheeks and she jerked her gaze back to his. "Wh-what?"

"The shirt. I could remove it...."

"No." *Yes.* But the kids...they could walk out anytime, and the last thing they needed to see was her and Rol going at it like a couple of bunnies. "Maybe later."

Besides, she wasn't ready for that again, yet.

Oh, yes, I am.

Rol was grinning. "If you change your mind...."

Damn tease of a man. What was happening here anyway? Last night they'd parted as friends. Confidants, with maybe a little unspoken desire for more, but in no hurry to rush back in. Now she was suddenly ready to jump his bones? Again.

But this time it wouldn't be about revenge or pain or anything except being with Rol. Being part of him, and his life.

She swallowed hard around her heart, which was suddenly beating in her throat. "Got any iced tea?"

Rol swirled the ice around the bottom of his glass. Iced tea was not what he needed at the moment, but he had gone along with Meryl's choice because…well, there was no reason. It had simply seemed right.

He cast a glance at the door to the communications room. Thirty minutes and Robyn's brood had not emerged. "I fear you will not get an opportunity to speak with Robyn."

The demands on the monarchs' time would start making themselves known soon. The process of integrating her into their society was a priority, after all.

Meryl waved her hand dismissively. "I can always come back later."

That she could. "You are always welcome. Would you like some more iced tea?"

This casual friendship talk between them was wearing. Friendship was not all he wished to share with her, but would she want a more serious relationship? Especially with one as deficient as himself?

"I'd love some more."

He shuttered the self-perceived innuendo and reached for the glass she handed him. There would be none of that next time. They would both be clear in their expectations and desires.

"Be right back." He strode toward the kitchen.

There was hope in his heart that there would be a next time. And there were no pressing matters for him to attend to on Bezchi at the moment, either. No reason to rush to win her over. Although, the issue of the missing elder remained. Maybe Meryl would be interested in joining him on a search for the wayward Kai Firewing.

Voices floated in from the common room. It sounded like Robyn's fledglings had emerged…which meant Meryl was going in and would not immediately need her tea. It also meant their quiet conversation was over. A twinge of disappointment plucked at his heart.

Now, for what reason should he be disappointed? It was not as though he would not have her to himself again later. And this was a perfect opportunity to get better acquainted with the younglings of his new monarch.

Robyn Raptorclaw. A good, strong name for a monarch…*his* monarch, as much as Kyzel was. He had judged her too harshly in the beginning, but thankfully had come to his senses before it had been too late. Now her family was his, and he would see after them for as long as he was on Earth.

He waved his hand over the sensor and a cabinet door slid up to reveal the glasses.

"So, that's the guy?" Kev's low-spoken question caught his attention.

"Yeah, that's him." That was Kathy's murmured response. Her voice was a bar higher than her sister's.

Karen's low chuckle came. "I still can't believe you helped Auntie Meryl do that."

Curiosity stirred and he tipped his head to one side. Do what? He should not use his superior hearing to listen in like a spy, but on the other wing, it was ingrained in him to do so. He *was* the prime advisor, after all. How else would he know how to advise his monarchs if he did not listen to those around him?

"Shh." That was Kathy again. "He has no idea, so don't say anything."

Kevin snorted. "Wish I'd been there to see her face when she realized everything had backfired on her."

"Next time you hack in," Karen murmured, "you should submit *your* name, Kat. If the old Bezchians are as hot as Rol and Kyzel, think about what the younger ones must be like."

"Oh, they are. Just wait until you meet Fyad...."

Rol grasped at the edge of the counter as shock ratchetted through him. Backfired...hack in...submit your name....

Great Aerie...it was Meryl *who submitted my name to the Silverstar Agency!*

Anger warred with amusement. How dare she? Yet the unexpected result of bringing them together could not be discounted. The question was, should he confront her about it or let her bring it up on her own?

"Hey, Rol."

He snapped his head up and met Kathy's blue-eyed gaze. The youngling stood in the arched opening to the kitchen, smiling. She must not have realized he had overheard. "Yes? Would you care for some iced tea?"

"That'd be great. Need help?"

"Of course." He waved his hand at the refrigerator. "Meryl put the pitcher in there. I will get more glasses."

She retrieved the iced tea and filled the glasses as he handed them to her. "Kev's going to grill you, you know."

He gave her a smile. "As he should."

"Oh, good." She appeared utterly relieved. "You're okay with that."

"I expect it." Such would be the case if they were Bezchian as well. He quirked one eyebrow. "Much like you wanted to do to Kyzel on your mother's behalf."

"Busted." She chuckled and grabbed two of the glasses. "Ready?"

"Do I have a choice?"

"No."

"I feared as much." He clasped the other two glasses in his hands. "Lead on, then."

By the time Meryl emerged nearly twenty minutes later, he and Robyn's brood were chatting amiably. At the whisper of the door opening, he turned to watch her move toward them with her usual fluid grace.

"I see Rol's still in one piece." She sidled up next to his stool, close but not quite touching.

Kev shrugged. "No idea what you're talking about, Auntie. We've been having a very nice conversation."

"Suuure."

Rol grinned at her. "I have enjoyed their company immensely."

The experience had not been so difficult. Almost pleasant. However, that did not mean he was not relieved it was over.

"Really?" Meryl slipped her fingers around his hand on the table. "I'm glad they went easy on you. But, there's a beach with our name on it, kids. Are you ready?"

The choruses of *yes* and *let's go* was accompanied by a mass exodus from the table. Once the glasses were cleared, the group moved toward the door.

Meryl paused in the doorway. "Are you sure you don't want to come with us?"

"I appreciate the invitation, but no." He cupped her lovely face between his palms. "This is your day. I will join Ms. Crawford at the negotiations for the afternoon."

An unidentifiable emotion crossed her face, then disappeared. "Okay. Call me tonight?"

He smiled down at her. "Absolutely."

She leaned a bit closer, closed her eyes and inhaled through her nose. That was odd. Different. Unexpectedly arousing. A flock of words rushed up, only to clog in his throat.

Before he could sort them out, she straightened and met his gaze. "Bye."

And then she was gone, her whispered word hanging in the air like a promise as the door swooshed closed. A smile tugged at the corners of his mouth. The knowledge of her covert actions with the agency was a discussion for later. She would eventually confess, in her own time. Pushing her on anything only led to her fighting an unnecessary headwind, and she had had enough of that in her life.

Besides, he was not as angry as he might have been had he found out a few days ago. He could wait. His Meryl was worth the effort.

FOURTEEN

What a day. Meryl stood at the breakfast bar and futzed with the roses Rol had given her the day before. He was special, that one. Just showing up out of the blue yesterday and coaxing her whole sordid history with Nathan out of her. Then forgiving her for being such a goddamn ass. Not to mention weathering an interrogation from her family at his age…what guy did that?

Except she hadn't told him about *everything* she'd managed to fuck up.

You gotta come all the way clean, girl.

And she would. She'd tell him about submitting the faked application to Silverstar tonight. Or the next time she saw him, whichever came first.

She drew her bottom lip between her teeth and raised her gaze to the darkened kitchen window. It was nearly eleven o'clock, and Rol wasn't keen about flying at night. Walking between her house and the Silverstar building was one thing, but walking from downtown L.A. to here…that was a bit overkill.

Raven Crawford's face rose up in her mind's eye.

Please don't let me be played for a fool again.

Raven was young and cute, but *not* a bimbo. And it was so easy to believe that Rol was smarter and more caring than Nathan. But she'd thought that about her ex too at one time.

And men think women are complicated?

Buzz.

She startled and inhaled a sharp breath at the sound of her doorbell. Who would be at her front door at this hour? She tiptoed to the door and peered out the peek hole. Two eyes, one gray, one blue, peered back. *Rol.* His chin was lowered and his mouth set with a sexy little smile.

God help her, how was she supposed to ignore all that? She gave the deadbolt a flick, then turned the knob. Now there was nothing between them—not even the screen door, which was mysteriously propped open with a flower pot.

"Good evening, Meryl." His voice sent a shiver through her.

"Hi." It was a breathless whisper, but at least she'd gotten the word out.

"May I come in?"

Hell yeah. She nodded and stepped back so he could contort his way inside. Watching him do that was almost as mesmerizing as watching him take off and fly.

Then he was inside, standing larger than life in her living room. Again. If he spread his wings out instead of holding them in close against his back, they'd almost span the width of the sixteen-foot room. The scent of him teased at her senses. She closed the door as she allowed her gaze to wander over the swaths of skin not covered by the strapped garment he called flying leathers.

Looks good, smells good....

He stepped closer, cradled her face between his hands, just as he'd done before she'd left his place earlier. "Sorry to visit so late."

"I'm not."

"Are the fledg...*kids* gone?"

She nodded, unable to look away from his unique eyes. "Left about twenty minutes ago."

"Good." The single whispered word seemed to hang in the air for an impossible moment, then he claimed her mouth with his.

A groan of pleasure rose from deep within her as his lips moved over hers. There was no fighting the attraction, the heat of desire, flaring in her core. She slid her arms around his middle, deepening the kiss.

The same molten need was back, and maybe a little stronger than before. God help her, this was going to happen again, but this time it would be different. This time she wanted Rol for Rol, not for revenge.

He pulled away, but not far. "Meryl?"

"Yes. And I mean it, Rol." She wrapped her fingers around the leather straps and took several steps backward, towing him along. "But in the bedroom this time, where it's just the two of us."

It took a moment for him to sidle through the bedroom doorway, but he seemed to be getting faster, and more confident about it. Then he unbuckled the flying leathers, tossed them in the corner, and tugged at the lacings of his pants.

She shooed his hands away. "That's my job, mister."

He didn't argue, just let his arms hang loose at his sides as she worked the laces, her fingers brushing the bulge underneath. Then she peeled his pants down, freeing him.

She gazed at his dick proudly standing erect from a thatch of flat, silky brown and gray feathers. It was similar to that of a sexually aroused human male, but there were evenly spaced, raised flesh-rings encircling its length. That was different.

"What do the bands do?"

"Bands?"

She touched her finger to one, and it fluttered.

Rol sucked in a sharp breath through his teeth. "They do that a lot when I release."

His words were choked with desire.

"So, *that's* what that was." They'd made her feel good, and based on his reaction, did the same for him. Double the pleasure. She met his gaze as she curled her hand around his length. "I felt them last time. It was mind-blowing."

And blew away other parts of her, too.

He rocked his hips forward, sliding in her loose grip. "Remove your clothing and get on the bed, Meryl. On your back."

Ooh, look who was taking charge. She gave him her sassiest grin, then did as he'd said, dropping her clothing on the floor as she went. This wasn't going to be slow, by any means, but it also wasn't going to be the wham-bam-thank you-ma'am like last time.

She lay back, sinking into the downy-soft quilt. Rol's hooded gaze raked over her body, from her face to her breasts, lingering on her snatch, then down to her legs—

which hung over the edge of the mattress from the knees down. A sweet dampness flowed from her. Good God, when was the last time that had happened without assistance?

He kneeled and spread her thighs apart. Anticipation stole her breath as he lowered his head. The touch of his tongue against her clit was almost too much, and she pushed her hips up, a keening cry escaping. He grasped her by her hips, holding her more or less in place as he sucked her nub in and nibbled.

"Holy fuck!" She came undone, straining against his hold even as she tried to arch closer, greedy for more.

Then she fell back on the bed, panting, as Rol lapped up her juices with slow, deliberate strokes. Already the delicious heat was building again. As if sensing that, Rol moved up, placing little kisses along her belly, lingering on her scar before continuing.

Finally, he closed his mouth over one nipple, swirling his magic tongue around it and sucking it in deep. If only she was more endowed. As it was, her chest was always practically flat when she lay on her back. Rol moved to the other breast without missing a beat, or making a comment, before lavishing attention to that one too. As if her lack in that area didn't bother him in the least.

The broad head of his dick nudge against her opening obliterating that line of thought. She raised her hips to draw him in, but he pulled away, then bumped her again. She tried once more, and again he moved away.

"Stop teasing and fuck me, Rol." She squirmed, but to no avail.

Suddenly, the world rotated, and she was face down on the mattress, ass in the air. Rol covered her with his warm body.

"How hard, Meryl?" he growled next to her ear.

Oh, thank you, God. "Don't stop until my eyes cross and I'm screaming."

His chuckle vibrated through his chest pressed against her back. Then, with one hard thrust, he was in her, filling her. Already his rings fluttered, a sign that he too was ready. He dug his fingers into her hips, holding her steady as he hammered into her. Her breathing turned erratic and she arched her back, taking him deeper.

A low growl from Rol was all it took to topple her over the edge, a scream escaping her throat. She clamped down on him even as he pushed deep, his release jetting into her so hard she felt it against her inner walls. His dick rings vibrated her right into another breath-stealing orgasm.

Then they collapsed together in a spent heap. There was no telling where she ended and he began, and it didn't matter.

But, damn, her eyes would probably still be crossed in the morning.

FIFTEEN

———◆———

Rol lay on his stomach, watching Meryl sleeping next to him under the shelter of his wing. The other wing was…somewhere. Hanging over the edge of the bed, if he had to hazard a guess. Hard to tell. Truth was, it could have fallen off and he would not care.

All that mattered was Meryl and the way her body snuggled against his. The golden glow of the morning sun illuminated her light brown skin. When had he ever felt so content? Satisfied? Happy?

The answer was, never.

It might be selfish, but thank the immortal ones that her first mate had left her. If he had not, then they would not be here now.

Ring.

The muffled sound of his cell phone came from the corner, where he had tossed his flying leathers. He frowned. Who would call him so early?

Ring.

"Shouyagetdat?" Meryl murmured.

"If it is important, they will leave a message."

Ring.

"Shpoken like a true Earthling." She giggled and blinked her beautiful hazel-green eyes open. "Morning."

He brushed his hand over her soft curls. "Good morning, beautiful."

Ring.

"Pfft. Not beautiful right now, but will be. Just as soon as I can move."

"Always beautiful."

"Don't argue with a lawyer."

A chuckle rumbled through him. "Good advice."

"I'll send you my bill later." She rolled onto her back and stretched her arms over her head with a loud yawn. "Between the kids yesterday and you last night, I slept so hard."

"Ah, yes. I did mean to ask you how was your day with Robyn's brood...kids?"

"Aww." She turned her head and met his gaze again, a happy sparkle in her eyes. "You're starting to sound like a local. Well, it was wonderful, even though my nose is sunburned."

He chuckled. "Tell me everything."

She did. Everything from walking the pier, to sunbathing on the warm sand, to the *hole-in-the-wall* seafood place they had discovered for dinner. The entire time, she dragged her fingers over his wings and through his feathers, an action that sent delicious tremors through him.

"We came back to my place for a movie and popcorn." A laugh bubbled out of her. "Then they all went over to Kathy's for a sibling slumber party."

"It sounds like an exceptional day."

"It was a great day. *Last night* was the exceptional part." She rolled closer and pressed her warm, luscious lips to the tip of his nose. "But, I've worked up an appetite and need to refuel before we do *that* again. Can I make you some breakfast?"

"I would love to eat." He too needed food because they were definitely doing more of *that*.

Ring.

He frowned. There was the phone again.

Meryl slid out of bed and grabbed a fluffy white robe off a hook inside her closet door. "You get that, and I'll get the food."

Ring.

It took him a few seconds of fumbling to find the cell phone in its pouch. He pulled it out.

Why is Ms. Crawford calling me this early?

He crouched on the floor, punched the green button with a finger, and brought the phone to his ear. "Is there a problem?"

"Well, good morning to you, too." Raven's tone was bemused. "Sorry to bother you, but yes, there might be a problem."

"What?"

"Have you spoken to Representative Chiraz in the last fourteen hours?"

"No." He rose and paced to the bed. "Why?"

"He didn't show up for the session this morning, and he's not in his room."

He turned and paced back to the corner. "Could he have gone for a fly…no, never mind."

It was impossible to get lost above Los Angeles. The Intergalactic Relations and Commerce buildings were very distinctive.

"No one's seen him since he left the fancy-shmancy dinner last night. Hold on…." There was a muffled exchange of words. "Okay, I'm back. The visiting Kam Ara delegation have offered to put some of their security staff in the air to search."

Ah, the Kam Arans to the rescue, one of the few other winged species in the Alliance. "Good. I will be there in thirty minutes. Keep me updated if anything changes."

"You got it."

He disconnected the call. None of this was good. First Elder Kai and Fyad disappear, now Chiraz Raptorclaw. Kyzel would flip his wings when he found out.

The savory scent of bacon cooking drifted into the bedroom. And even worse, now he had to tell Meryl he could not spend the day with her after all.

He blew out a harsh gust of air. Nothing good would come from delaying the inevitable. He dressed quickly and made his way to the kitchen.

Meryl looked up from her position in front of the stove, stirring a panful of liquidy, yellow eggs. "There you are— uh, oh. I'm guessing that phone call wasn't good news."

"It was not." He leaned against the tall breakfast bar. "It seems the Raptorclaw representative on the Bezchian negotiation team is missing."

Her eyes widened. "What? How?"

"No idea." He rubbed his hands over his face, a vain attempt to wipe away the stress. "I regret I must go deal with this matter, Meryl. Ms. Crawford is far from qualified to handle it on her own, though she will try."

"Why would she do that?"

"Because she is aware that I am testing her, but she is not sure for what reasons. So, she may use this as an opportunity to try and impress me."

Her gaze returned to the pan, but not quick enough to hide a flash of fear.

"Meryl." He leaned farther over the counter and waited until he had her full attention. "My hope is that she will work for the Raptorclaw clan, not for me. A youngling like her could do so much better than that heinous publication she is with, would you not agree?"

The corners of her mouth twitched upward with a poorly suppressed smile. "Yes. I'm pretty sure she isn't as tough as she acts." She pointed to a glass of orange juice on the bar. "Well, at least drink your O.J. before you go off to save the universe."

The tart-sweet citrus drink was another Earth beverage he had come to appreciate. And, a much better choice at this early hour than hard cider.

"Thank you, but...." He tucked his wings in close to his back, and stepped around the tall eating counter. The kitchen was tiny, at least in his estimation. He reached for Meryl and drew her against his chest. "I would rather drink you."

The spatula slipped from her grip and clattered onto the stovetop. That was invitation enough for him.

He dipped his head and claimed her lips, savoring the

sweet taste of her before drawing back. "And that is my promise to you for when I get back."

Her mouth opened and closed, but no words came out. If he had known that was how to render her speechless, he would have kissed her like that the first day they had met by Robyn's hedge.

"Not all males are like your former mate, Meryl. *I* am not like him." He stepped back. "I will call you when I am able, *kee duotok.*"

With that, he headed toward the front door, and the problem of the missing representative.

The antique mantle clock chimed twice and Meryl gave it a narrow-eyed glare. Just what she needed, a reminder that yet another hour had gone by and Rol still hadn't called. Had he eaten lunch? How long did it take to find a full-grown Bezchian anyway?

She tossed the legal thriller she'd plucked off her bookshelf onto the coffee table. Having read it before took the suspense out of it anyway. She should've gone to Solvang with the kids instead, dammit.

The tune of *Hit the Road, Jack* blared from her phone.

That'd be Rol. Well, shit, she should probably reprogram *that* ringtone. Things had changed between them a little bit.

Kee duotok. She'd looked it up, and it meant *my air current.* It was used exclusively as a term of affection between lovers.

She smiled as warmth blossomed in her chest, then gave

the green icon on her phone screen a quick tap. "Hello?"

"I have come to regret not waiting for those eggs." The growl of his voice sent a pleasant shiver through her.

A laugh slipped out. "And the bacon."

"And the orange juice," he lamented.

"Well, big guy, you're in luck because it's all the fridge, waiting for you." She leaned back into the sofa cushions. "Any luck finding your missing representative?"

"Yes, but I almost wish we had not."

"Why? What happened?"

A long sigh from his end brought an image to mind of his wings drooping. "He disappeared on purpose, and now that he has been found, he is withholding his support of any trade agreement with Earth."

"Can he *do* that?"

"Bezchian trade law seems to support his stance." Another sigh. "And it gets worse. Representative Odu Firewing is considering following suit. He is awaiting word from the clan's Most Esteemed Elder, Uri Firewing. If the Most Esteemed approves it, the negotiations are off. And, unfortunately, that is what I expect will happen. The Firewings are ancient in their ways, and do not handle change very gracefully."

Well, shit. "What about the Firewing monarchs? Do they have any say?"

"Uri is their leader. The Firewing clan is the only one who does not have monarchs. It is complicated to explain."

"So, there's no way around it? No loophole?"

"If there is, I do not know of it. Raven is working on a media release worded to put pressure on them to come back to the table, but I have my doubts."

"Well, if anyone can do it, she can." Which, at the moment, was about the nicest thing she could say.

You're one suspicious bitch, Meryl Faulkner.

It wasn't that she really *believed* Rol would be attracted to Raven, it was just that this was too similar to a movie she'd seen before. And it scared her more than a little bit.

"I know." His tone of resignation made her heart ache for him. "I wish I had a stronger air stream to ride, though."

"I understand, Rol. I wish the same."

And I wish I could go down there and help.

But there wasn't anything a retired divorce lawyer could do in this situation. Nobody was fighting over who got the house, and there were no custody battles to wage.

"That means more to me than you imagine, kee duotok. Thank you."

And just like that, he'd reminded her that she meant something to him. She was important, valued.

"You're welcome, babe." She needed to think of something better than that to call him, but babe would work for now. "Call me when you are on your way back. I'll have dinner ready."

"I miss you."

She couldn't suppress the smile at the sincerity woven into his words. "I miss you, too."

After disconnecting, she stared at the phone, tapping it thoughtfully with one red fingernail. The reason she and Nathan had been so successful in their law practice was mostly because of the hours she spent researching, looking for loopholes. She'd *loved* that aspect of her career.

Rol's situation wasn't family law, but research was research, right? How difficult could it be?

Of course, he hadn't actually asked her to get involved, but tough. It couldn't hurt to look. If she didn't find anything, then he'd never know she'd snooped. But, if she did....

That was it. She was doing the thing. She hurried down the hallway to her office at the back of the house and fired up her computer.

SIXTEEN

———————●———————

Rol held the cell phone up to his ear as he glared through the glass window at the single occupant of the session room. Chiraz Raptorclaw, the most stubborn pain in the wing in the galaxy, had locked himself in and now refused to speak to his own prime advisor. Rol jabbed a finger in the direction of the phone within Chiraz's reach on the table, a silent demand that he pick up the handset. The other man shook his head slowly.

A growl of frustration rumbled in his throat. Chiraz had forced this issue, and now would not speak? Fine, then. The male could sit in there until the universe ended.

He thumbed the cell phone's red disconnect button and shoved the device back into its pouch attached to his flying leathers. At least he did not need to explain the disappearance of Careene's brother to Kyzel now.

No, but I will have to explain why the trade negotiations are on the brink of failure.

Currents of air, his reputation as a competent and successful negotiator was in danger of becoming tarnished.

He pinched the bridge of his nose between his thumb and forefinger. It was well after dinner time, and fast approaching bedtime. He should find a private room and call Meryl to let her know he would be at least another hour.

"Prime Advisor Rol."

He turned his attention to the red-capped, red-winged Bezchian striding toward him. His gut tightened at the approach of his other problem. "Representative Odu, or is it Elder now?"

Odu came to stop and glanced in the window at Chiraz. "It is still Representative." He shifted his golden-eyed gaze to meet Rol's. "Most Esteemed Elder Uri is not eager to open trade with Earth, yet his orders are for me to continue as an open-minded representative for the Firewing clan."

That was an unexpected positive turn of the storm. "And what about you? How do you feel about continuing?"

"Do my personal feelings matter, Prime? Do any of ours? Or are we servants to the will of the Alliance?"

Fair point. The Alliance *did* encourage trade between its planet members. Sometimes going as far as to assert pressure to see it done. Clearly, change did not sit well with the phoenix.

Ring.

The sound of Rol's phone filled the tense silence. He glanced in Chiraz's direction. The male's attention was fixed on a wide rectangle of translucent white light floating in the air above the tabletop, not the phone. His eyes tracked lines of lettering invisible from Rol's position. The Alliance's technology was more advanced than the computers and monitors still widely in use on Earth, something else that must change.

One problem at a time.

Ring.

Rol retrieved the phone from its pouch and held it up. Ah, Meryl. A smile tugged at the corners of his mouth and he accepted the call.

"Hello, Meryl."

"Hey, I found it!" Her voice had a breathless quality, as though she had been running.

"Found wh—"

"Gotta show you. I'm downstairs at the east entrance, but security won't let me in."

He frowned. "You are *here*? At the Intergalactic Relations and Commerce?"

"Yes, Einstein." She laughed. "And I have something that might help with your situation up there, but you need to come get me. And hurry."

"Be right there." He disconnected and met Odu's questioning gaze. "Excuse me, Representative. There is something I must attend to."

He took off down the hallway at an undignified trot, wings trailing behind him, heading for the bank of lifts that would take him the closest to the east entrance. Even though the Intergalactic Relations and Commerce building was a twenty-four-hour entity, the lifts were not crowded at this time of night, and neither was the ground floor atrium.

He made his way toward the security checkpoint, searching for Meryl's golden curls.

There she is.

Pacing on the other side of the guards' station like she had energy to burn. That was his Meryl.

She snapped around as if she had sensed him, and smiled. "That was fast."

"You said to hurry." He spread his arms as he strode toward her, and she stepped into his embrace. Ah, but she felt good pressed against him. "Besides, I was eager to see you."

The breath of her chuckle caressed the exposed skin at the base of his neck, just above the top strap of his flying leathers. He curved his wings around her, cocooning them in privacy.

After a moment, she pushed back and patted the leather satchel hanging over her shoulder. "I printed it out, but I still want to show you on a computer—or whatever tech they have here—just in case there are any questions about its authenticity."

"What is it?"

"Not here." She glanced around the lobby as though spies could be hiding behind one of the tropical trees. "I'm probably overreacting, but I'd rather be safe than sorry."

"Of course." Discretion was an admirable trait. "This way."

It took a few minutes to get her cleared by security, then upstairs into a private session room with tech access.

She pulled a piece of paper out of the satchel and handed it to him. "Read the highlighted section."

His gaze was drawn to the words marked with a yellow line, as the tapping of her fingers against the keyboard projection filled the silence.

...with no exception, unless there is a blatant conflict of interest on the part of the Objectee, and there is a qualified, readily available replacement....

"What is this?"

"A get-out-of-jail-free card courtesy of the Degen vs. Fokazi case brought to the Alliance's judicial chambers in Galactic Common Time Year 6954."

Of course it was, how foolish of him. "It is 7564 now."

"More than six hundred years later." She flashed him a small smirk. "And, more importantly, it has never been contested, nor overturned. Ever. It's like everyone forgot about this one little line over the last six centuries."

"And a similar issue never arose again, until now." At least to the best of his knowledge.

"Here's the ruling in its entirety." Meryl waved her hand at the image floating in front of her. "I'm hoping it means the same in the original language as it does in the English translation."

He bent to scrutinize the document, scrolling up then down. Utterly amazing. It seemed solid enough.

"And then there's this." She flicked her fingers over the keyboard image again, and Chiraz's history came up. "Voila, instant personal conflict. Kyzel mated an Earthling—something the brother of his deceased mate has publicly castigated him for. You didn't tell me Chiraz was Careene's brother."

"It never came up, but I apologize for the oversight." He turned to half-sit on the table facing her. "I am in awe, Meryl. You may have single-handedly saved the Bezchi-Earth trade negotiations. I would have never thought to look for a legal ruling. It does concern me that this is not mentioned in the Alliance's trade rules, but that can be changed later."

He would make certain of it.

She shrugged her slim shoulders. "Extensive research experience, a simple keyword search, and being fluent in legalese. Turns out that intergalactic law is not so different from Earth's."

"And that is why it would have taken me years to find it."

"Don't sell yourself short, Rol. I know you would've figured it out. I'm just hoping you know someone here who qualifies to take Chiraz's place."

"Me."

Her mouth popped open. "You?"

"I have negotiated on behalf of my monarchs for thirty-eight sun migrations." One of his many duties as prime advisor.

"Oh, well. I guess that settles it, huh?"

He tucked his finger under her chin and dipped his head to claim a kiss. "Thank you."

Her sudden grin lit her face and she tipped her head with the sassy air he loved. "Anything to get you back home with me."

SEVENTEEN

———— ✦ ————

One thing that could be said about shit hitting the fan: the fallout was pretty instantaneous. Meryl smoothed her hand over the crisp linen of her gray pantsuit—the one she'd loved to wear when she'd had to represent a client in court—and lowered herself into a corner chair. Next to Raven. Because, why not? The girl hadn't done anything wrong, and after observing her during the morning session, it was clear she had no designs on Rol.

Look at me being all confident and sure.

It was liberating to have blown away that cloud of suspicion. Rol didn't deserve it, and neither did Raven.

The reporter looked up from her notes and grinned conspiratorially. "Didn't I tell you this corner was the best seat in the house?"

"Yes, you did. Thank you." Avoiding notice had been her primary goal all day. She jerked her chin in the direction of Raven's notepad. "Want to review what you've got so far?"

"That'd be great, if you don't mind." She flipped back a few pages. "Let's see...your discovery confirmed by

Alliance legal experts. Rep. Chiraz unofficially relieved of duty by the Bezchian Intergalactic Trade Guild. Prime Advisor Rol to be unofficially recognized as his replacement, and a hiatus for the negotiations to be called this afternoon while both of them go back to Bezchi to be officially castigated or recognized. Anything else?"

"What…no mention of my fashionably trendy business attire, hand-delivered by my goddaughter at the butt-crack of dawn this morning, risking life and limb in the Sunday morning gridlock?"

Raven snort-laughed quieter than Meryl had ever seen anyone do before. Which was just as well, since the meeting had just been called back in session.

Her gaze drifted to Rol, standing in the middle of the room responding to questions and proclaiming his willingness to accept the responsibilities of a Bezchian trade guild representative. The lighting in the room highlighted the sharpness of his features, but there was a real softie under that tough exterior. He was so damn handsome.

And he's leaving.

Oh, sure, he'd be back to do his part for the negotiations once he was made the official representative, but would he have any time for her?

An elbow-nudge brought her attention back to Raven.

The reporter leaned closer and handed her a slip of paper folded in half. "I just got a text from unfortunately-still-my-boss at *Blast off!*. Would you give this info to Prime Advisor Rol?"

"Sure."

"Thanks. Later." Raven gathered up her stuff and slipped

out pretty much unnoticed, which was a rare talent for someone who liked to dress outside social norms. At least, on Earth.

Meryl grinned to herself. The kid was growing on her.

When the session broke, signifying the beginning of the hiatus that would end once Rol returned from Bezchi, she rose from her seat. Rol was already making a beeline toward her, and that was enough to fill her heart with light.

He claimed his usual kiss from her and led her to the elevators. Once on board, she handed him Raven's note, which she hadn't even been slightly inclined to peek at. Trust may not be something she gave easily, but Rol had earned hers.

He scanned the note, his grin widening. "Raven has a lead on the whereabouts of Elder Kai and Fyad. She will be in contact as soon as she knows more."

"That's great." She eyed the ascending numbers. "Why are we going up, not down?"

His eyes sparkled with mischief. "I have a surprise for you."

Ding.

The doors opened and organic scents from the rooftop atrium wafted in. "On the roof?"

"Yes." His smile faded into seriousness and he licked his lips.

What? Was that nervousness from Mr. Confident himself?

He tugged her hand, gently, and she followed him off the elevator, past security, and outside onto the roof. A cool breeze, carrying the scent of the ocean, danced over her skin.

The landing and takeoff platform stretched out about thirty feet before an abrupt drop off. Beyond that, the city of Los Angeles and the shimmering blue Pacific Ocean.

It was breathtakingly gorgeous in the afternoon sunlight. "This is where you come and go from the IRC?"

"Yes, it is." He cleared his throat. "You of course heard that I must accompany Chiraz back to Bezchi?"

"Yeah." She lowered her gaze to the toes of her black flats. "I heard that part."

"I…." He coughed. "I wondered if you would like to come with me?"

She snapped her gaze up to his. "Seriously?"

Oh, please don't let this be a dream.

"Very much so."

"*Aaah.*" She launched herself at him, wrapping her arms around his neck. "Yes, yes, *yes*. I'd *love* to go with you, Rol."

His warm, relieved chuckle washed over her as his arms tightened around her. "Then we will go to your house so you can pack. After that, I must stop at Silverstar and ask Ms. Vogel to keep the suite open in case Elder Kai and Fyad return. Then, we will go to the galactic spaceport just before sunset to board our ship."

"Tonight?" *Of course tonight, genius.*

"Yes. The sooner we go, the sooner we can return to Earth. Now." He bent and scooped her into his strong arms. "Are you ready?"

"Whoa…what are ya doing?"

"Preparing to fly."

Did her heart just stop beating? "But…wait…no…my car is in the garage."

"It will be safe. We will not be gone for more than a week."

"But." She gave the takeoff pad a narrow-eyed glare. "Are you out of your fucking mind?"

There. She'd said what she was really thinking. Jumping off a fifty-one-story building was *not* on her bucket list.

"Not at all. I am proving that I am a spontaneous loose-ass."

"A *what*?" Oh, God. This was all because she'd called him a tight-ass the day Robyn left?

The insane off-worlder started toward the all-too-close edge, each step faster than the last.

She tightened her grip around his neck and pressed against him as close as humanly possible. The faint rumble of the traffic so far below seemed louder. A scream clawed its way from her chest to her throat. She was going to die.

Then Rol hurdled into empty space. Her scream broke free and followed her over the edge as gravity grabbed them, because gravity *always* won.

Fwump. Fwump. Fwump.

The sure sound of Rol's wings beating the air was a welcome alternative to the swoosh of air rushing past her ears as they'd plummeted toward the street below. And, they were rising.

"Was that so bad?" Rol practically purred the words in her ear.

"Can we go back and get my stomach? I think it's still on the roof." Along with her heart. "I think I shit my pants, too."

Rol laughed, and suddenly everything was okay. "Your stomach will catch up. And do not worry, Meryl, I will always have you."

Aw. What more could a girl ask for? Except maybe a case of adult undergarments.

Earth receded like a jewel set against a piece of the blackest velvet imaginable. So black it was like staring into infinity; into the past, present, and future all at once.

Meryl pressed one palm, then the other, against the cool, smooth window viewer, and leaned in until the tip of her nose touched the glass. If she concentrated, she could feel the barest vibration from the ship's engines.

"Now I understand what the astronauts meant by the overview effect."

"Is this a good thing?" Rol murmured his question against her neck.

"Very good." Better than that, but *amazing* seemed too ordinary. "Magnificent. Awe-inspiring. My God, Rol, I never dreamed I'd see Earth like this."

"And I never dreamed I would be able to hold you like this, in this place." He pressed his lips to her earlobe. "Thank you for coming with me."

"Mm." As nice as his attentions were, they needed to wait. She turned in his embrace and looked him square in the eyes so she wouldn't chicken out, again. "There's something I gotta tell you. Something I should've told you before."

A haze of uncertainty dimmed the sparkle in his eyes. "What?"

"Well." She ran her tongue over her lips. "It was me. *I* submitted your name to the Silverstar Agency."

His mouth curved up in a grin. "I know."

"Uh, you do?" *How* could he know?

"It was not too hard to figure out. Especially after I overheard Robyn's brood talking about it in the common room a couple of days ago."

A snort popped out. Well, duh. Of course it'd be the kids. It just figured. "Are you mad?"

He seemed to study her entire face before shaking his head. "No."

That was a relief. "Good. Because now I'm *glad* I did it."

"I am, as well." He took a step back and wrapped his large hand around hers. "Since we are in confession mode, come sit with me. There are things you should know."

"Well, that sounds ominous." She padded after him through their quarters—which were at least the size of half a football field—to the fully reclined lounging bench-thing in the middle of the room.

There wasn't anything he could say that'd change her mind about being here with him. Being in love did that to a person.

One corner of her mouth twitched upward as she sat facing him. In love. Yes, that was it, she was in love with this caring, handsome, and often stubborn off-worlder, and she should probably tell him.

Rol took a seat next to her, arranging his wings so the ends hung over the opposite edge of the bench. He seemed to be fussing to get them in just the right place. Either that or he was nervous about something, which was so unlike him.

Finally, he rested his clasped hands on his knees, drew in a deep breath, then exhaled. "Meryl, you are the best gift I have ever received. But, you must know by the colors of my eyes that I carry weakened genes and am not a fit mate for anyone. Still—"

"Wait a minute." She frowned. "Who told you *that*?"

"It is common knowledge." He shrugged, the knuckles of his hands turning white. "This is why I was never mate-matched. Why I have no siblings. Why my father immersed himself in his work and grew increasingly distant from my mother and me."

"Oh, that is *such* bullshit. What kind of person does that to their own kid?" His father, obviously. What a jerk. "Look, Rol, I *love* the colors of your eyes. They're unique and beautiful, just like you." She placed her palms to his smooth cheeks. There was a cautious sort of hope reflected in those eyes. "And here's another thing…I love you."

He blinked once, twice, his mouth hanging open. "You do?"

"Yes. I do."

A slow, silly, full-faced grin replaced the stunned expression. "Meryl, will you be my life mate?"

"I—"

"Wait. You need to know that we raptors mate for life. I will never leave you, and there will never be another for me. It is not possible."

Was he for real? Because, if he was, her heart was damn well going to explode. And other parts of her too. A guy who would never pull a Nathan on her for the rest of their lives—and beyond, apparently? "But, what if I die?"

"I will not survive without you."

"Oh, stop being so dramatic." She batted at his chest. "Kyzel remated."

He covered her hand. "Kyzel is not me, and I am not being dramatic. I have lived my whole life believing there was no mate for me, only to find you. You proved me wrong…you proved the elders wrong. *You* are the one who *I* love, who holds my heart. If you go, you will take my heart with you. And where my heart is, is where *I* will be."

"If anything happened to you, I think it'd kill me, too." She wiggled her hand around in his grip and closed her fingers around his. "I choose you too, Rol. Will *you* be *my* life mate?"

"*Always.*" He packed the word with such fierceness, everything down south turned molten.

Then she was plastered against his body, his arms and wings around her before it had registered in her mind that he'd moved. And, damn if that wasn't exactly where she wanted to be, wrapped up in him, breathing in his scent.

Minus the tears, which seemed to have overridden her usual femme-faucet protocols. "I'm soaking your shirt."

"I have others." His grip on her loosened a little. "Unless your wish was to get me out of this one."

A watery laugh bubbled up. "Maybe."

"Anything you wish, kee duotok." He was back to nuzzling her neck.

"Anything?"

He pulled back slightly and she raised her gaze to meet his. "Anything."

"What do you have in mind, big guy?"

The light touch of his fingertips against her jaw sent a shiver down her arms. "Maybe a little of this." He brushed his lips over hers. "And this."

"Yes." She breathed out the word.

"How about this?" He deepened the kiss, his tongue searching for hers as a moan rumbled in her throat.

She opened her mouth to meet his slow, languishing, incredibly sexy kiss. Her focus on anything but him was lost, letting him set the pace for now. This time there was no reason to rush; not yet, anyway.

She let her fingers do the walking up the sides of his omlek, giving each lace a tug until all of them were undone. Then she wiggled her fingers through the openings and traced them over his muscles.

It was wicked, the contour of his muscles. Wicked and delicious, like the way his hands now lifted the hem of her shirt. She moved back to give him some space and shimmied her arms out of the sleeves. Then Rol sucked her bottom lip in and nibbled at it before letting it go with a wet pop.

Clothing came off in a flurry of motion until they came back together, standing naked, except for her thong. Lips sealed, slow and steady gave way to urgent and needy. The only way she could get enough of him was if she crawled into his skin. And maybe not even then.

Rol pushed against her, and she took a step backward, then another, and another until the backs of her legs bumped against the bed.

"Mm." She pulled back. "Wait."

"What?" He peppered urgent little kisses to her chin, cheeks, eyes.

"You first."

He raised his head and blinked at her in adorable confusion.

She gripped him by the biceps and moved, turning him one-eighty. "On the bed, big guy."

Confusion faded into a slow grin of anticipation, and he sat on the bed. "I think I like where this is going."

He reached for her, but she danced back a couple of steps. "Ah, ah, ah. Remember I said you first. Now lay back…all the way. That's it."

Exactly how she wanted him, flat on his back, wings spread across the largest mattress she'd ever seen. She climbed onto the bed, crawling on hands and knees until she could look down at his magnificent bit of manhood.

"Oh, honey." She lowered herself and ran her tongue from base to tip.

Rol's entire body quivered and his hands closed around fistfuls of the top cover.

His low growl sounded like a green light to continue. She repositioned herself, then took him into her mouth, playing her tongue along those devilish little ridge rings. The hiss of air through teeth came from somewhere above, and she moaned her own satisfaction at the salty taste of him.

Even here he had that allspice scent, faint, but all his musk. She closed her hand around his base and sucked in as she moved back up his hard shaft. Rol said something she couldn't understand, but it wasn't *stop*, so she kept bobbing and sucking over his fluttering rings.

"Stop, Meryl." His fingers in her hair stilled her. "I want to come inside a different part of you."

The *different part* of her clenched in anticipation. Yeah, she wanted that too. She released him, kicked off her thong, and settled herself over his hips.

God, the way he looked at her, all sexy with that hooded gaze, how had she not jumped his bones the first time they met? "You ready for this?"

"More than you know." The hungry gleam in his eyes confirmed his words.

She stroked his length, rubbing her folds over his rings as a groan of pleasure slipped out. Then she rose up, guided him to her entrance, and sank down on him. The sense of stretching bit by bit to accommodate him was sensual enough for her eyes to roll back. This just got better and better every damn time.

She reached his base and a soft sigh escaped her. "God, Rol."

"Do not stop, Meryl." He nudged his hips up. "I need you."

He had handed over control to her, and that was so fucking sexy. She braced her hands against his chest, slid up his length and back down. Rocking, riding him faster and faster as a sweet tension built inside her channel. And those rings already fluttering, hitting her G-spot with uncanny accuracy.

"Rol…." So close….

He gripped her hips with an almost bruising force and thrust up with a grunt, lifting them both off the bed. Then a second time. The third time, her dam broke and she clamped down around him hard. She leaned back taking him deeper, and screamed her release to the ceiling.

On his next thrust, his roar of satisfaction joined hers, sending her into a second wave as the rings expanded, titillating her. And still they didn't stop. The little buggers coaxed three more orgasms out of her before allowing her to collapse, spent, on Rol's heaving chest.

A profound sense of contentment and wellbeing surrounded her. Along with the familiar scent of allspice. Rol wrapped his arms around her as his heart beat under her ear. This was the way she wanted to go to sleep every night, and wake up every morning. With this imperfect, ornery off-worlder who had somehow slid right into a Rol-shaped hole in her heart.

Damn, but her golden years were going to be fun.

To my dear readers,

Whew! Writing Meryl and Rol's story was a blast. They are a fun couple, and I hope you enjoyed reading about their adventure as much as I did writing it. If so, please take a moment to leave a review, or at least some stars.

Next up, *Trial by Fire*. Yes, our favorite match-makers find love as well! Check out the sneak peek below.

Happy reading!

~Lea Kirk

*Please turn the page
to enjoy an excerpt from*

Trial by Fire
Silverstar Mates

Elder Kai Firewing tread light-footed along the path to the meditation garden, alert for the presence of others in his clan. The sun-warmed Bezchian desert sand pushed between his toes with each step, a familiar comfort that did not soothe his anxiety today. He should not be here in this oasis at the center of his colony. The meditation garden was for deserving elders, and he was not deserving. Had not been so for the last fifty-five sun migrations.

A puff of a breeze flitted over his bare chest, rustling the lightweight fabric of his billowing yellow leggings. He flattened his lips into a straight line. How had everything gone so wrong so suddenly? For more than three lifetimes, he had excelled at matching mates for the four mortal clans of his home-world. Had joined families that would thrive together, be stronger in their collective attributes. Fulfilled his role in the ancient Bezchian tradition upheld by the elders of the Firewing clan: the long-lived phoenixes.

One day he had been fine. The next, every couple he had attempted to join lacked…something. An element, a spark, a flame of the heart…something utterly unnecessary to a successful mating. Yet its absence had crippled his ability to unify any couples, over and over, until Most Esteemed Elder Uri had stopped giving him assignments. That decision still stung worse than a fire wasp. But Uri was the eldest of the elders, and had the final word in such decisions.

Still, the memory of that missing element left a bitter taste in Kai's soul.

Seventy-three sun migrations into your third incarnation, and you are as useless as a sand roach.

He had been *born* to match mates. His failure to do so—multiple times—was tantamount to a scandal. He ground his teeth together. The elders of the Firewing clan had a reputation to uphold, by the air currents. How did such a *malady*—because there was no better word to describe it—happen to an otherwise young, healthy phoenix?

"Greetings, Elder Kai." The soft, murmured words snapped Kai from his thoughts.

A fledgling-sized elder approached from around the fountain at the garden's center, her golden-eyed gaze on the ground instead of meeting his.

He pulled his wings in close to his back, the tips of his primary feathers brushing the backs of his leggings, and gave her a respectful nod. "Greetings, Elder Ena."

Even though she presented as no more than ten sun migrations, she was older than him by three hundred, thanks to the miracle of rebirth every one hundred sun migrations. Some in the Firewing clan had lived as long as two thousand sun migrations. It was understandable why off-worlders were often confused by this, and hence the reason his kind preferred the solitude of the Bezchian deserts.

"May your meditations be insightful." Ena quickened her pace as she passed him, her red and orange leggings molding to her spindly legs with her burst of speed. No doubt eager to avoid conversation with one as fallen as he.

"Aye, and your matches always strong." As his once were.

Ena continued along the path, and Kai turned his attention to finding an available white stone meditation perch to sit on. There, the one snuggled between two ember-berry bushes seemed to be waiting for him. And it would be in the full sun for a while. His current form was not of an age to regenerate yet, but was old enough to appreciate the heat provided by Bezchi's star.

He settled on the warm stone, pulled up one leg at a time to sit cross-legged—not an easy feat for his aging body— and sighed out loud in bliss. The stone's heat penetrated the wispy fabric of his leggings and eased into his muscles. He rested his hands on his knees and closed his eyes. The familiar sensation of calm settled over him as he slipped into a trance.

The trick now was to connect with his own elusive inner peace through his nearly four lifetimes of memories. Easier to anticipate then to achieve, as usual...but wait. There was something...wavering mirages of green. *That* was different. There was not much that was green in the desert.

The mirages solidified into...bushes? Yes, they were bushes dotted with some sort of deep red, layered flowers unlike any he had ever seen before. He lowered his gaze to the ground under his feet. Also green and lush in a way that his home was not.

A large, stone-lined pond materialized several paces ahead, at the farthest end of which was a fountain of water spraying upward before falling back down in misty droplets. He should be able to hear its soft pattering, but only complete silence pressed against his ears. It was odd, and somewhat disconcerting.

What is this place?

An answer to that question seemed unlikely without so much as a hint of enlightenment or familiarity from this vision.

A patch of air between him and the pond shimmered and morphed into a figure, similar to a small Bezchian female, but without wings. How odd. He studied her from behind. The garment covering her form was most unusual. A lacey, cream colored, body-hugging sheath of some sort. It clung to her curves, flaring over her shapely backend and full hips, before ending mid-calf.

Why was he sharing this space with one clearly not of his world? She had not yet noticed him standing behind her; her attention seemed focused on the pond. He really should not engage her, but an impulse too strong to ignore urged him forward. She drew him like a desert moth to a flame-spider's glowing web, one tentative step at a time.

The bubbling sound of the fountain reached his ear, finally coming to life for no apparent reason. And bird song. Not a lot, but there were clear chirps emanating from the tall, droopy tree on the pond's opposite shore.

His attention was riveted on the sprays of tiny white flowers woven into the female's brown...what *was* that on top of her head? Not headfeathers, obviously. Whatever the soft-looking strands of silk were called, they were elegantly swept up into some kind of fastener. Something deep inside him stirred, a strange aching around his heart that all but stole his breath.

Who is *she?*

He must see her face. Must hear her voice. Must touch her, because all that would be enough to explain why he was here in this place with her.

He reached out one hand toward the graceful curve of her shoulder.

The soft intake of her breath echoed in his ears, and she straightened as if she had sensed him.

"Who's there?" Her whispered words were odd, foreign, yet he understood.

He stopped, frozen by indecision. Should he touch her, or wait for her to turn around? She was already turning her head, the soft curve of her jaw holding his gaze, a breath away from revealing her face....

.

Want more out of this world love?

Hitch a ride on the Intergalactic Dating Agency's space
ship to romance! Our friendly author-pilots will take you
on adventures you will never forget.

Now boarding here:
RomancingTheAlien.com

About the Author

USA Today Bestselling Author Lea Kirk loves to transport her readers to other worlds with her science fiction romance books. She's the author of the award-winning Prophecy series, and the rollicking romantic Silverstar Mates series about seasoned SFR love, that's part of the Intergalactic Dating Agency series. Why? Because sexy has no expiration date!

Ms. Kirk lives in California with her wonderful hubby, their five kids (aka, the nerd herd), and a spoiled, bossy, yet somehow adorable, pup.

LeaKirk.com

www.ingramcontent.com/pod-product-compliance
Lightning Source LLC
Chambersburg PA
CBHW051835170626
46807CB00003B/1187